BETWEEN TWO SKIES

BETWEEN TWO SKIES

JC CRAWFORD

LIBERTY HILL PUBLISHING ELITE

Liberty Hill Publishing
555 Winderley Pl, Suite 225
Maitland, FL 32751
407.339.4217
www.libertyhillpublishing.com

© 2024 by JC Crawford

All rights reserved solely by the author. The author guarantees all contents are original and do not infringe upon the legal rights of any other person or work. No part of this publication may be reproduced, distributed, or transmitted in any form or by any means, including photocopying, recording, or other electronic or mechanical methods, without the prior written permission of the author, except in the case of brief quotations embodied in critical reviews and certain other noncommercial uses permitted by copyright law.

Due to the changing nature of the Internet, if there are any web addresses, links, or URLs included in this manuscript, these may have been altered and may no longer be accessible. The views and opinions shared in this book belong solely to the author and do not necessarily reflect those of the publisher. The publisher therefore disclaims responsibility for the views or opinions expressed within the work.

Paperback ISBN-13: 979-8-86850-560-7
Ebook ISBN-13: 979-8-86850-561-4

TABLE OF CONTENTS

Chapter 1: The Everyday Unraveled................1
Chapter 2: Anomaly in the Sky 5
Chapter 3: The Message..........................9
Chapter 4: The Summoning......................13
Chapter 5: The Connection.....................17
Chapter 6: Descent into Chaos 21
Chapter 7: The World on the Brink 27
Chapter 8: Into the Abyss 31
Chapter 9: The Silence and the Storm 35
Chapter 10: The Interrogation 39
Chapter 11: The Departure 43
Chapter 12: Humanity's Edge 45
Chapter 13: The Unraveling.....................47
Chapter 14: Beyond the Event Horizon 51
Chapter 15: Revelations of Eloxon 5 57
Chapter 16: The Chosen One 61
Chapter 17: The Mind's Horizon 67
Chapter 18: The Return and the Revelation........77
Chapter 19: The Veil of Intentions................85
Chapter 20: The Genesis of Utopia...............93

Chapter 21: The World's Crossroads	101
Chapter 22: The Threshold of Intent	107
Chapter 23: A New Dawn Within the Dome	113
Chapter 24: The Siege of the Dome	119
Chapter 25: The Power Unleashed	125
Chapter 26: The Council of Shadows	131
Chapter 27: The Will of Eloxon 5	137
Chapter 28: The End of an Era	145

Chapter 1:
THE EVERYDAY UNRAVELED

In the heart of suburban tranquility, Elijah "Eli" Jacobson lived a life that was the epitome of the American dream. A sturdy figure with a keen eye, Eli's presence was both comforting and commanding. At thirty, he had achieved more than most would in a lifetime—a loving wife, Amanda, whose brilliance as a doctor was only matched by her warmth, and three children who were the center of their world.

Desirae, the middle child at seventeen, was a mirror image of her father, both in intellect and compassion. Sarah, nineteen, had just started college, carrying with her the family's legacy of determination and grace. And then there was Elijah Junior, an eleven-year-old bundle of curiosity and energy, always following a step behind his father, eager to learn the ways of the world.

Eli's work as a security contractor was shrouded in secrecy, a necessary veil for the sensitive nature of his projects. His days were a blend of routine and unpredictability—mornings spent reviewing reports and evenings filled with family dinners and bedtime stories. Yet, beneath the surface, his mind was always alert, always planning for the next mission that could take him anywhere across the globe.

The Jacobsons' life was a delicate balance, a dance between normalcy and the shadows of top-secret endeavors. Amanda's steady hand kept the family anchored, her hospital shifts often aligning with Eli's sudden departures and unexplained absences.

But one ordinary day, the fabric of their reality began to unravel. A black hole, no larger than a compact car, appeared in the sky, positioned ominously between the Earth and the Sun. It was a cosmic anomaly that defied explanation, its gravitational pull distorting the sunlight into a celestial spectacle.

As the world's governments and scientific communities scrambled to understand this unprecedented event, the black hole began to communicate. Radio waves, pulsing like the heartbeat of the universe, reached out towards Earth, carrying a message hidden in numbers.

The sequence was baffling: 01071984, 312659875, 32.7767, 96.7970. To the untrained eye, they were random, but to those who knew how to listen, they spoke volumes. They were the birth date, social security number, and ever-changing coordinates of one man—Elijah Jacobson.

The revelation sent shockwaves through the corridors of power. How could a cosmic entity, a void in the very fabric of space, hold such intimate knowledge of a single individual? The questions multiplied, and with them, the urgency to find answers.

Eli's world was turned upside down as government agents arrived at his doorstep, their faces etched with a seriousness that mirrored the gravity of the situation. With his family's bewildered eyes upon him, Eli was whisked away to a place where the line between science fiction and reality blurred.

Chapter 2:
ANOMALY IN THE SKY

The morning sun rose as it always did over the Jacobson household, casting a warm glow through the curtains of Eli's home office. He sat there, surrounded by the quiet hum of his computer equipment, reviewing the latest encrypted files from his last assignment. The work was meticulous, requiring a sharp mind and an even sharper instinct for the nuances of national security.

Amanda was already at the hospital, her shift starting just before dawn. The house was still, save for the soft footsteps of Desirae and Sarah preparing for school, their voices a distant murmur as they discussed the day ahead. Elijah Junior was curled up on the couch, lost in the pages of his favorite comic book, his imagination running wild with tales of heroes and villains.

It was a scene of domestic bliss, a snapshot of a life that Eli had worked hard to build and protect. But as he glanced out the window, his eyes caught a glimpse of something that sent a chill down his spine. The sun, the giver of life, had a shadow cast upon it—a black spot that defied logic.

News alerts began to flood his phone, each one more urgent than the last. A black hole, a tear in the very fabric of the universe, had appeared in the sky. It was small, almost insignificant against the vastness of the cosmos, but its presence was undeniable.

The world held its breath as scientists and astronomers raced to their observatories, their instruments trained on the celestial intruder. Governments convened emergency meetings, their leaders grappling with the potential threat looming overhead.

Eli's instincts kicked in. He knew that this was no ordinary event, and his role as a security contractor might soon intertwine with the unfolding drama. He reached for his phone, ready to make the necessary calls, when the first of the radio waves hit.

The signal was strong, a clear pattern emerging from the static. Numbers—dates, sequences, coordinates—streamed across the screens of monitoring stations worldwide. The message was cryptic, yet targeted, a beacon that seemed to point directly at Eli.

As the realization dawned upon him, Eli felt a sense of foreboding. His life, his identity, was being broadcast from a phenomenon that should not exist. The implications were staggering, and the questions it raised were even more so.

Anomaly in the Sky

Why him? Why now? And what did the black hole want with Elijah Jacobson?

As the sun dipped below the horizon, casting a fiery glow across the sky, the black spot remained, unwavering and enigmatic. The townspeople of Crestview, who had spent the day oscillating between fear and fascination, began to retreat to the comfort of their homes, but Eli remained rooted to the spot, his gaze locked on the celestial anomaly.

"Why him? Why now?" The questions circled in his mind like moths around a flame. The black hole, a phenomenon that should have been a mere specter in the vastness of space, felt personal, as if it had chosen this moment, this place, to appear.

Eli's thoughts were a whirlwind of confusion and curiosity. He had always felt a strange connection to the cosmos, a pull towards the stars that he could neither explain nor ignore. And now, with the appearance of the black hole, that connection seemed to manifest into something tangible, something that beckoned him.

As darkness enveloped the town, the black spot became even more pronounced against the twilight sky. It was as if the universe had opened its eye, and its gaze was fixed solely on Eli. The air around him grew charged, a static hum that raised the hairs on his arms.

"What do you want with me?" Eli whispered into the night, half-expecting an answer from the void.

The black hole remained silent, but in that silence, Eli felt a resonance, a vibration that coursed through his very soul. It was a call to action, a summons that he could not ignore. The black hole wanted something from him, something only he could provide.

Chapter 3:
THE MESSAGE

The world was in a frenzy. The black hole's message had been decoded, and its contents were as baffling as the phenomenon itself. The numbers were a direct link to Elijah Jacobson. It was a puzzle that defied explanation, a cosmic riddle with a human focal point.

Eli sat in a secure conference room, the walls lined with screens displaying the black hole and the data it had emitted. Government officials, military personnel, and top scientists filled the room, their faces etched with concern and curiosity.

The discussion was heated, theories flying as fast as the coffee poured. Some believed it was a message from an extraterrestrial intelligence, a first contact scenario straight out of science fiction. Others argued for a more terrestrial explanation—a sophisticated prank or a new form of cyber warfare.

But for Eli, the situation was deeply personal. The numbers were his life, reduced to digits and broadcast for all to see. He felt exposed, vulnerable in a way that his years of training had never prepared him for.

As the debate raged on, a voice cut through the noise. Dr. Lena Kovalenko, a leading astrophysicist, had a different take. She spoke of quantum entanglement, of connections that transcended space and time. Her theory was wild, unproven, but it resonated with Eli. There was something about the black hole that felt familiar, as if it were a part of him.

The room fell into a hushed silence as Dr. Kovalenko elaborated on her theory. "If we consider the black hole not just as a gravitational anomaly but as a bridge," she posited, "then perhaps what we're seeing is a message that's been entangled with Mr. Jacobson's very existence."

Eli's heart raced. The idea that his life was somehow quantumly linked to this cosmic phenomenon was both thrilling and terrifying. It suggested a destiny that had been written in the stars long before he was born.

As the meeting adjourned, Eli was approached by a group of officials who spoke in hushed, urgent tones. "We need to understand the connection," they implored. "You may be the key to interpreting this message and what it means for humanity."

In the days that followed, Eli underwent a series of tests—scans, interviews, and examinations by top scientists and cryptographers. Each test seemed to deepen the mystery rather than solve it. The numbers were undeniably tied to him, but how and why remained elusive.

Eli sat in the sterile confines of the government facility, the relentless hum of machinery a constant reminder of the extraordinary situation. The black hole's message had become an obsession, the numbers a riddle that consumed his every waking thought.

The team of experts, a collection of the finest minds from around the globe, worked tirelessly. Cryptographers, astrophysicists, and linguists pored over the data, searching for patterns and meanings within the cosmic call. Yet, the numbers remained an enigma, a sequence that defied conventional understanding.

As the coordinates continued to shift, leading to disparate points across the Earth, Eli felt a growing connection to the black hole. It was as if it spoke to him, a voice from the void that only he could hear. The numbers were personal, a cosmic beacon that had singled him out for reasons unknown.

Amanda's face haunted his thoughts, her worried gaze a stark contrast to the calm demeanor she always presented to the world. Desirae's inquisitive nature would have made her an invaluable ally in this puzzle, her mind as sharp as any cryptographer's. Sarah's steadiness, her ability to remain composed under pressure, was a trait Eli found himself leaning on, even in her absence. And little Elijah Junior, with his boundless energy, would have filled the room with questions, his innocence a light in the growing darkness of uncertainty.

The facility became a second home, a place where coffee cups piled up, and the passage of time was marked only by the changing of the guard outside the door. Eli's life, once defined by the predictable rhythms of suburban existence, had been upended. Now, he lived moment to moment, each tick of the clock a step closer to an answer or a step further into the abyss.

Eli found himself at the center of a whirlwind of activity. The black hole's message had turned him into an object of global significance. Yet, amidst the chaos, he felt an unshakeable calm. There was a part of him that had always known his life was not entirely his own, that he was part of something greater.

Chapter 4:

THE SUMMONING

The world had changed overnight. The black hole's message had turned Elijah Jacobson from a private security contractor into the most talked-about man on the planet. His name was whispered in the halls of power and shouted across the airwaves, a symbol of humanity's sudden brush with the unknown.

Eli's home, once a sanctuary, was now a fortress. Government agents patrolled the grounds, their eyes watchful for any threat that might emerge from the sky or the street. Inside, Amanda and the children tried to maintain a semblance of normalcy, but the tension was palpable.

Amanda, ever the pillar of strength, held her family close, her medical training providing a calm in the storm. Desirae and Sarah were resilient, their youthful optimism a counterpoint to the gravity of the situation.

And Elijah Junior, though confused by the chaos, found solace in his father's steady presence.

But Eli was far from steady. The numbers—the message—haunted him. They were a beacon that had singled him out for reasons he could not fathom. And now, the government wanted his help to unravel the mystery that had bound his fate to the cosmos.

Director Barnes was a man of few words, but his message was clear. Eli was to accompany him to a facility so secret it didn't exist on any map. There, the best minds in the world would work with him to understand the black hole and its intentions.

The journey was a blur, a swift passage through checkpoints and secure corridors. Eli was briefed on the way, told of the theories and fears that had gripped the world. But no theory could explain why the black hole had chosen him, why it whispered his name across the void.

The facility was a labyrinth of technology and secrecy, nestled in the heart of an undisclosed mountain range. As Eli was ushered through its sterile halls, he couldn't help but feel like a specimen under a microscope, studied and probed by the very people who sought his aid.

In a high-security briefing room, Eli was introduced to a team of experts assembled from around the globe—astrophysicists, cryptologists, military strategists—all united by the enigma of the black hole. They turned to him with a mix of reverence and desperation, as if he held the key to unlocking the universe's secrets.

Director Barnes, with his hawk-like gaze, made it clear that the stakes were higher than any of them could imagine. "Mr. Jacobson, the message you carry could be a turning point for our species," he said. "We need to understand its origin, its purpose, and why you are at its center."

Eli listened to their theories, each more outlandish than the last. Some suggested the black hole was a natural cosmic recorder, echoing back Earth's own signals. Others speculated about alien civilizations using advanced technology to reach out across the void.

But as the hours stretched into the night, a startling hypothesis emerged from Dr. Kovalenko. "What if the black hole is not just a messenger but also a gateway?" she proposed. "A bridge created for someone—or something—to cross over to our world?"

The room fell silent, the implications of her words hanging heavy in the air. Eli felt a chill run down his spine. The familiarity he felt with the black hole, the sense of being called to it, suddenly took on a new, profound meaning.

The silence in the room was palpable, each person grappling with the implications of Dr. Kovalenko's hypothesis. Eli, feeling the weight of countless eyes upon him, knew that the answer lay within his grasp, yet just beyond reach. The black hole's message was a puzzle, and he was the missing piece.

As the night wore on, the team dissected every possible angle, every scientific theory that could shed light on the black hole's purpose. Eli, however, felt a pull towards a different kind of understanding, one that transcended science and delved into the realm of the metaphysical.

"Perhaps it's not just about where the black hole is leading us, but when," Eli mused aloud. The room turned to him; their attention rapt. "What if this gateway is a bridge through time as well as space? What if it's calling me to witness something crucial, something pivotal to the human race?"

The team pondered Eli's words, the idea resonating with a strange sense of possibility. Time travel was the stuff of science fiction, yet here they were, facing a phenomenon that defied all known laws of the universe.

Director Barnes, a man who had seen his fair share of mysteries, nodded slowly. "We need to be prepared for any eventuality," he declared. "Eli, we'll support you in whatever comes next. You have the full backing of this facility and the government."

Chapter 5:

THE CONNECTION

The facility was a hive of activity, a nerve center where the worlds brightest gathered to solve the puzzle of the black hole. Screens lined the walls, data streaming in real-time, a digital symphony played out in numbers and graphs.

Eli was introduced to the team, a diverse group of scientists, engineers, and analysts. Each one greeted him with a mix of respect and curiosity, aware of his unique connection to the phenomenon that had brought them all together.

Dr. Kovalenko was there, her eyes alight with the thrill of discovery. She spoke to Eli of quantum threads, of the fabric of reality that bound all things together. Her words were a comfort, a suggestion that there was order in the chaos, a pattern to be found.

But as the days passed, the connection between Eli and the black hole deepened. The numbers continued to follow him, shifting with his every move. It was as if the black hole was watching, waiting for something only Eli could provide.

The government was anxious, their desire for answers growing more desperate. They turned to Eli, pressing him for memories, for any clue that might explain the link. But Eli's past was a closed book, his projects classified, his knowledge compartmentalized.

The connection was clear. The black hole was not just a messenger; it was a mirror, reflecting the life of Elijah Jacobson back at him. And the key to understanding it lay within him, in the experiences and secrets he had locked away.

As Eli watched the sequence of images, a narrative began to unfold, one that told the story of his life in reverse. From the man he was now, back through the milestones of his life—his marriage to Amanda, the birth of his children, his early years in the security field—all the way to his first memories as a child.

The images were not just a playback but an invitation to introspection. Eli saw the moments that had defined him, the decisions that had steered his path, and the people who had shaped his character. It was as if the black hole was peeling back the layers of his existence, urging him to look deeper.

With each passing image, Eli felt a growing sense of purpose. The black hole was communicating in the most personal language possible—the language of his own history. It was showing him that the answers he sought about the universe were intertwined with the truths of his own life.

The breakthrough was more than scientific; it was existential. Eli realized that the black hole was not an external force acting upon him but a reflection of something intrinsic within him. It was a part of his being, a cosmic counterpart to his earthly self.

The revelation was profound, and as Eli continued to watch the images, a sense of understanding began to dawn on him. The black hole was not just a cosmic anomaly; it was a conduit for a message that transcended time and space, a message meant for him.

Eli's life, it seemed, had been a tapestry woven with threads of an otherworldly origin. The moments that had seemed coincidental, the dreams that had felt too real, the inexplicable knowledge he possessed—all were pieces of a puzzle that was now coming together.

The team around him watched in awe as Eli interacted with the data stream, his intuition guiding him to make connections that the most sophisticated algorithms had missed. It was as if he was speaking a silent language, one that bridged the gap between human and the divine.

As the last image faded, Eli stood up, a resolve in his eyes that had not been there before. "I know what I need to do," he said, his voice carrying a new timbre of authority. "The black hole—it's a gateway, and I'm the key. It's time I step through it." But, could I, do it? Could I leave my family behind and journey into the unknown. I may never see them again.

The scientists protested, citing the unknown dangers, the potential for a one-way journey from which there was no return, but the government officials had already made up their minds. Elijah will be sent into the black hole. The orders coming down from the very top. Eli will make the journey whether he wants to or not.

Chapter 6:
DESCENT INTO CHAOS

The black hole, once a scientific curiosity, had become a harbinger of doom. The government's attempts to probe the enigmatic void had failed spectacularly. Drones, satellites, even unmanned spacecraft—each one was torn asunder by the black hole's insatiable hunger, leaving no trace behind.

The world watched in horror as the experiments escalated to the unthinkable. Animals, sent as living test subjects, met the same fate. The message was clear: the black hole was a one-way journey to oblivion.

Panic spread like wildfire. The streets were filled with protestors and preachers, each voicing their own theory about the black hole. Some saw it as a sign of divine judgment, others as a portent of an alien invasion. The chaos was palpable, the fear infectious.

Governments struggled to maintain order, but the fabric of society was fraying. Riots erupted in major cities, looters taking advantage of the unrest. The stock markets plummeted, and emergency services were overwhelmed.

In the midst of this turmoil, the President made a decision that would change the course of history. Elijah Jacobson, the man at the center of the mystery, was to be sent into the black hole. It was a mission with no return, a sacrifice in the name of understanding and perhaps saving the world.

Eli's refusal was firm. He could not abandon his family, could not leave his children fatherless. But as he watched the world descend into madness, his resolve wavered. The black hole had chosen him, and perhaps it was his destiny to face it.

Eli's mind was a tempest of emotion as he held his family close, their warmth a stark contrast to the cold uncertainty of the void that awaited him. Amanda's eyes, brimming with unshed tears, searched his for reassurance, for a sign that everything would be alright. Desirae and Sarah clung to their father, their silent strength a testament to the bond they shared. And Elijah Junior, with a bravery that belied his years, looked up at his father, his small hand gripping Eli's with a trust that was both humbling and heartbreaking.

The President's decision had sent shockwaves through the corridors of power, the gravity of the situation dawning on even the most stoic of officials. Eli Jacobson, once an anonymous figure in the vast machinery of government security, was now the lynchpin in a narrative that spanned the stars.

The black hole, a specter in the sky, had become a symbol of humanity's fragility, a reminder of the thin veneer of control that civilization held over the forces of the universe. The failed attempts to probe its depths had only served to heighten the fear, each lost drone and satellite a dirge for mankind's hubris.

As the world teetered on the brink, the streets became a canvas of chaos. Protests erupted outside government buildings, the populace demanding answers that no one had. Preachers took to the pulpits and the airwaves, proclaiming the black hole to be a divine retribution for humanity's sins. And amidst the cacophony of fear and speculation, the voice of reason was drowned out.

Eli watched the news reports, the images of cities in turmoil a stark reminder of what was at stake. The stock markets had become a barometer of panic, their precipitous drops reflecting the collective fear of an uncertain future. Emergency services, stretched to their limits, battled to maintain a semblance of order as the fabric of society unraveled.

In the quiet of his home, now a fortress against the world's madness, Eli wrestled with the enormity of the President's request. To venture into the black hole was to embrace the unknown, to sacrifice himself on the altar of curiosity and, perhaps, hope.

Amanda's voice broke through his reverie. "Eli, you can't do this," she pleaded, her hands cupping his face. "Think of the children, think of us."

Eli's heart ached with the weight of his decision. He knew the risks, understood the likely finality of his journey. But as he looked into the eyes of his family, he saw not just the fear but the love, the unspoken belief that if anyone could face the abyss and return, it was him.

The night before his departure was a vigil of whispered promises and shared memories. Eli recounted stories of his childhood, of the dreams that had always felt too real, too vivid to be mere figments of his imagination. He spoke of his love for Amanda, for the life they had built together, and for the children who were his heart and soul.

As dawn broke, casting a pale light on a world holding its breath, Eli donned the suit that had been prepared for him—a marvel of engineering designed to withstand the unimaginable forces that awaited him. The fabric felt like a second skin, a barrier between him and eternity.

Eli stepped onto the platform that would transport him to the black hole's threshold. His family stood behind the safety glass, their faces a mosaic of pride and sorrow. Eli turned to them, his hand pressed against the glass, his eyes conveying a silent message of love and farewell.

With a deep breath, Eli stepped into the void, the black hole's call resonating in his soul. The world watched as the man who had become their reluctant hero disappeared into the maw of the unknown, a solitary figure against the backdrop of infinity.

Chapter 7:
THE WORLD ON THE BRINK

The news of Eli's decision spread quickly, a glimmer of hope in the darkness. The world, on the verge of collapse, clung to the story of the man who would brave the unknown for the sake of humanity.

But the hope was tinged with despair. Religious leaders spoke of end times, their words echoing through the halls of worship and the crowded streets. Cults emerged, worshiping the black hole as a deity, their rituals dark and desperate.

The governments of the world united, if only in fear, their resources pooled in preparation for Eli's journey. The black hole had become the common enemy, a threat that transcended borders and ideologies.

Eli's training began, a rigorous regimen designed to prepare him for the impossible. Scientists and engineers worked around the clock, constructing a vessel that could withstand the journey, or at least deliver Eli to the event horizon.

Eli suiting up, the vessel ready for launch. His family stood by, pride and sorrow etched on their faces. The world held its breath, waiting for the moment when Elijah Jacobson would become the first human to confront the abyss.

As the news of Eli's decision rippled across the globe, it brought with it a wave of collective anticipation. The world, teetering on the precipice of chaos, found a focal point in the narrative of one man's courage. Eli Jacobson, once a guardian of secrets, was now the bearer of hope, a lone voyager on a path that no one else could tread.

The atmosphere was electric, charged with the energy of a thousand emotions. In the streets, the masses gathered, their eyes skyward, their hearts beating in unison with the ticking clock that counted down to Eli's departure. The black hole, a silent watcher in the heavens, was a reminder of the fragility of existence and the audacity of hope.

Religious fervor reached a fever pitch as leaders of faith grappled with the implications of the black hole. Some saw it as a test of humanity's resolve, a divine challenge to be met with prayer and penitence. Others declared it the end of days, a sign of the final reckoning. And amidst the cacophony of prophetic declarations, new cults rose, their devotion to the void a dark mirror to the fear that gripped the world.

Governments, once disparate entities divided by ideology and ambition, found common ground in the shadow of the black hole. Resources were pooled with a singular focus: to support Eli's mission. The black hole, a threat that recognized no nation or creed, had become a unifying force, a common adversary that demanded a united front.

Eli's training was an odyssey in itself, a grueling series of simulations, physical trials, and mental challenges that pushed him to the limits of human endurance. The vessel, a marvel of engineering wrought from the collective genius of Earth's greatest minds, was a testament to the will to survive and explore. It was designed to navigate the uncharted waters of space, to carry Eli to the edge of the known universe and, perhaps, beyond.

The night before the launch, the world seemed to hold its breath. The streets were silent, the air thick with the weight of the moment. Eli's family, a portrait of stoic pride and raw emotion, stood beside him as he donned the suit that would shield him from the void's embrace.

Amanda's eyes were a wellspring of strength, her love a beacon that outshone the darkness. Desirae and Sarah, their faces a blend of their mother's resolve and their father's determination, held each other close, their bond unspoken but unbreakable. And Elijah Junior, his young face a canvas of mixed fear and admiration, looked up at his father, the hero not just of his own story, but of a tale that would be told for generations to come.

As Eli stepped into the vessel, the hum of machinery and the murmur of voices faded into the background. He was alone with his thoughts, his doubts, and his resolve. The hatch closed with a finality that echoed in his heart, the sound a punctuation mark at the end of one chapter and the beginning of another.

Chapter 8:
INTO THE ABYSS

The day of the launch arrived. The skies were clear, the black hole a stark contrast against the blue expanse. The world's eyes were on Eli, his every move broadcast across the globe.

The vessel was a marvel of engineering, a sleek pod designed to pierce the heavens. Eli climbed aboard, his heart steady, his mind focused. He had said his goodbyes, made peace with his fate.

As the countdown began, a hush fell over the crowd. The engines roared to life, a crescendo of hope and fear. And then, with a burst of fire and light, Eli was launched into the sky, his trajectory set for the heart of the black hole.

The journey was surreal, the stars streaking past as he approached the event horizon. The black hole loomed larger, its darkness an all-consuming void.

Eli's thoughts turned to his family, to the life he was leaving behind. He recorded a message, his final words, a testament to his love and his courage.

The vessel, a solitary speck against the cosmic tapestry, hurtled towards the unknown. Inside, Eli Jacobson, once a man rooted to the Earth, now found himself a voyager on the frontiers of human exploration. The cabin around him was silent, save for the hum of the engines and the soft whir of computers. It was a silence that spoke volumes, filled with the echoes of humanity's quest for knowledge and the unspoken fears of what lay ahead.

Eli's hands moved over the controls with practiced ease, the result of countless simulations, but nothing could truly prepare him for the reality of this moment. The black hole, a celestial maw, awaited him—a gateway to either enlightenment or oblivion.

As the vessel neared the event horizon, the point of no return, Eli felt a profound isolation. He was alone, a single consciousness bearing the collective hopes and terrors of his species. The instruments before him began to behave erratically, their readings fluctuating wildly as the laws of physics started to unravel.

Eli's mind wandered to his family, to Amanda's unwavering support and the bright futures he hoped for his children. He thought of Desirae and Sarah, their laughter, their dreams, and young Elijah Junior, whose curiosity about the universe mirrored his own. The message he recorded for them was a declaration of love and a hope for their understanding. "I do this for you, for us, for the future," he spoke into the recorder, his voice steady despite the turmoil within.

The black hole now filled the viewport, a swirling abyss that defied comprehension. Eli could see the stars bending around it, their light twisted and dragged into the darkness. It was beautiful and terrifying in equal measure.

As the vessel crossed the event horizon, a shudder ran through its frame. Eli braced himself, his body tensed for an impact that never came. Instead, there was a moment of utter stillness, as if the universe itself had paused to draw breath.

Then, with a suddenness that took Eli's breath away, the darkness gave way to light. Brilliant, blinding light flooded the cabin, and Eli shielded his eyes with his arm. When he dared to look again, what he saw was beyond imagination.

The vessel had emerged into a place that was neither here nor there—a nexus of reality, where the fabric of space-time folded upon itself. Colors unseen by human eyes danced before him, and the stars—oh, the stars! They were countless, a sea of diamonds on a canvas of eternity.

Eli's heart raced with a mix of fear and exhilaration. He had done it; he had crossed into the abyss and emerged on the other side. But where was he? Was this a different universe, a parallel dimension, or something else entirely?

Chapter 9:
THE SILENCE AND THE STORM

For five years, the world held its breath. The black hole that had appeared so suddenly and taken so much had vanished, leaving behind a sky that seemed emptier for its absence. Nations retreated behind their borders, economies crumbled, and fear became the currency of the day.

Amanda Jacobson and her children became figures of quiet resilience, their nightly ritual of writing letters to Eli—a beacon of hope in a world darkened by uncertainty. They gazed at the stars, each one a distant sun, wondering if one of them was watching over Eli.

The government's efforts to reach out into the void where the black hole once resided continued in vain. Probes and signals were sent, piercing the cosmos with humanity's longing for answers, but the universe remained silent.

Then, without warning, the silence was shattered. A brilliant light erupted in the void, a white hole where the black one had been. It was a cosmic reversal, an expulsion where there had once been only absorption.

From this white aperture emerged a vessel, reminiscent of the one that had carried Elijah Jacobson into the unknown. But it was altered, adorned with structures and technology that spoke of an intelligence far beyond Earth's own.

The ship's arrival sparked a flurry of activity. The military cordoned off the Nevada desert, a barren expanse now the stage for humanity's second encounter with the extraordinary. Scientists, leaders, and the world's media descended upon the site, each seeking to be the first to witness the next chapter in this cosmic saga.

The ship sat in silence; its intentions inscrutable. For two days, the world waited, a collective breath held in anticipation. Amanda and her children were there, at the forefront, their eyes never leaving the vessel that might hold the answers to their prayers.

Elijah Jacobson's return was not the triumphant homecoming the world had hoped for. As he stepped out of the ship that had brought him back from the abyss, the government's welcome was cold steel and suspicion. The military, weapons drawn, surrounded him, their faces masks of fear and caution.

Eli had changed. The years in the void had reshaped him, not just in mind but in body. He appeared younger, healthier, as if the very essence of life had been distilled within him. His beard was neatly trimmed, his hair perfectly styled, and his eyes sparkled with a vitality that belied his ordeal.

He smiled, a gesture of peace and familiarity in a situation that was anything but. "I have missed home," he said, his voice carrying across the tense air. But his words were met with orders, not embraces. The government saw not a hero, but a potential harbinger of unknown threats.

As Eli complied, laying on the ground to be handcuffed, his family watched from afar, hidden in a bunker for their protection. The reunion they had dreamed of was snatched away by the hands of caution.

The world's media circled above, their helicopters buzzing like a swarm of curious insects, capturing every moment of the unfolding drama. The sight of Eli, once a symbol of hope, now treated as a possible enemy, sent ripples of shock and confusion across the globe.

Scientists approached the ship, eager to unlock its secrets and understand the advanced technology that had returned Eli to Earth. But an invisible barrier thwarted their efforts. The ship was impenetrable, a silent guardian of the knowledge it held within.

Eli, being led to an interrogation chamber, the weight of the world's fears pressing down upon him. The ship remained in the desert, a monument to the unknown, its mysteries locked away behind an unseen shield.

Only Eli could provide the key, but at what cost? Would the government's fear override their humanity, or would they listen to the man who had journeyed beyond the stars?

Chapter 10:

THE INTERROGATION

The interrogation chamber was a stark contrast to the boundless expanse Eli had traversed. The walls were close, the air heavy with suspicion. Government officials, unseen behind the two-way mirror, watched as Eli was hooked up to a polygraph machine, the rhythmic beeping a metronome to the tension in the room.

Eli's demeanor was serene amidst the clinical coldness of his surroundings. The bright light overhead cast deep shadows across his face, but it could not darken the clarity in his eyes. He was a man who had seen beyond the veil of reality, and the games of fear and control played by those in power held no sway over him.

"Where is my wife? My children?" he asked, his voice steady. The question hung in the air, unanswered, as the interrogators pressed on with their own agenda.

"Where have you been?" they demanded, their voices a mix of authority and desperation.

Eli's confusion was genuine. "It has been ten years for me," he replied, his words sending ripples of bewilderment through the observers. The doctor scribbled notes, the pen scratching loudly in the silent room.

The interrogation chamber, a cold and sterile room designed to extract truths, became a battleground of wills. Eli Jacobson, the man who had faced the abyss and returned, sat in silence, his demeanor an unyielding fortress against the barrage of questions.

"Mr. Jacobson, we need answers," the lead interrogator pressed, his patience fraying at the edges. "The world is in chaos. You sit here with the knowledge that could save us all, yet you choose silence?"

Eli's response was measured, his voice a calm counterpoint to the growing agitation around him. "All will be revealed when the time is right," he stated, a mantra that offered no satisfaction to the desperate men and women seeking to pierce the veil of mystery he represented.

The officials behind the two-way mirror exchanged uneasy glances, their discomfort palpable. The silence that Eli offered was more disconcerting than any confession or revelation. It was a silence that held power, that hinted at truths too vast for the confines of the room.

As the hours ticked by, the interrogators' tactics grew more confrontational, their questions sharper, more demanding. "Are you a threat to national security, Mr. Jacobson?" one asked, his voice hard as stone. "Is there something out there we should be preparing for?"

The Interrogation

Eli remained unmoved, his eyes betraying none of the storm that raged within him. "I am no threat," he replied, his tone even. "But there are forces at play that are beyond any one nation's control. Forces that demand our unity, not our division."

The frustration in the room reached a boiling point, the air charged with a mix of fear and anger. "You speak in riddles," another interrogator accused. "If you have any loyalty to your planet, to your species, you will speak plainly. What did you see? What do you know?"

Eli's gaze swept over the faces before him, each one a mask of fear masquerading as strength. "I have seen the fabric of the cosmos," he said, his voice a whisper that cut through the tension. "And I have learned that our fate is not written in the stars, but in the choices, we make here, on Earth."

The officials began to demand answers more fervently. The began to demand access to the ship. Questioning Eli on what he is hiding behind the walls of that machine.

The demand for access to the ship was met with a calm refusal. "I will not let anyone enter," Eli stated, his tone leaving no room for negotiation. "I will tell you everything you need to know, but when the time is right." Eli began to shift in his seat attempting to stand up.

The officials insisted he was not free to leave, but Eli's gaze pierced through the mirror, locking eyes with the General on the other side. The officials puzzled, He can't see us, can he?" "I can see everything," he said, and the fear that gripped the officials was palpable. It was a declaration of power, a subtle shift in the balance that had once favored those behind the glass.

Chapter II:

THE DEPARTURE

The interrogation chamber had become a crucible, the air thick with tension and the sharp scent of fear. Military personnel flooded the room, their orders echoing off the walls, weapons trained on the solitary figure of Elijah Jacobson.

Eli's calm was an oasis in the chaos. "I don't know why I expected better treatment," he mused aloud, his voice a stark contrast to the cacophony of demands. "They told me you all would act this way upon my return."

The questions came like a barrage, a storm of curiosity and dread. "They? Who are they?" "Are you referring to aliens?" "Where were you?" The inquiries merged into a single, desperate plea for understanding.

But Eli was done with words. With a simple raise of his hand, silence fell like a curtain. The soldiers, their weapons still raised, retreated, their bravado crumbling under the weight of the unknown.

Then, with a gesture that spoke louder than any command, Eli pointed. The soldiers' bodies went limp, their weapons clattering to the ground, a symphony of surrender to the inexplicable power that Eli wielded.

As he walked out of the building, untouched and unchallenged, Eli touched his earlobe, speaking into the void. "Prep the ship, I am getting my family, and we are going back," he said, his voice carrying the finality of a door closing.

A voice, distant yet clear, questioned his resolve. "Are you sure? You know what that means for them? You said you wanted to save all of them, not just your family."

Eli's response was a whisper of resignation. "They are all the same. Maybe it was a mistake to even come back here."

Chapter 12:
HUMANITY'S EDGE

The world outside the bunker was a maelstrom of fear and confusion. The appearance of the white hole, followed by the arrival of Eli's ship, had tipped the scales of global unrest into outright pandemonium. Governments teetered on the brink of collapse, their authority challenged by the unexplainable events unfolding in the sky and on the ground.

As Eli exited the facility, he was met by multiple government vehicles filled to the brim with Suit wearing officials. One of them stepped out and proceeded to open the back door to the vehicle. Out of the vehicle cam Amanda who immediately ran into an embrace with Eli.

Eli and Amanda stood amidst the chaos; a moment of personal reunion overshadowed by the larger crisis at hand. Their embrace was a fleeting sanctuary, a reminder of what was at stake—not just the fate of one family, but the future of all humanity.

Amanda began to hammer thousands of questions to her Husband. It has been an eternity for her. She had not known if Eli was alive or dead.

Amanda's questions were a torrent, but Eli's gentle hush was a dam against the flood. "I will tell you everything," he promised, his voice a steady anchor. "Just get the kids, and we can leave."

The government officials encircling them were a wall of resistance, their faces set in grim determination. "Your children are safe," they assured, but their refusal to divulge more sparked a fire in Amanda's eyes. "Was I a trap?" she accused, her voice rising in anger. "You can't keep my family from me!"

The agents stood their ground, unmoved by the pleas and protests. "Tell us what we need to know, and then you and your family can leave," they demanded, their ultimatum hanging in the air like a guillotine blade.

The world watched; its collective breath held in suspense. The chaos that had once simmered now boiled over. Riots erupted in city streets, and doomsday cults proclaimed the end of days. The fabric of society, already threadbare, was tearing at the seams.

Eli's gaze swept over the scene, taking in the armored vehicles, the tense faces of the agents, the distant sounds of unrest. He knew the power he held, the knowledge he possessed, could be a beacon or a bomb. The choice was his.

Chapter 13:

THE UNRAVELING

As the agents awaited Eli's decision, the chaos outside grew. The streets were filled with the cacophony of a civilization in turmoil. The riots had spread like wildfire, the flames of fear fanned by the winds of the unknown.

Religious zealots proclaimed the end times, their fervent cries rising above the din of society's collapse. Governments, once pillars of order, now clung to power by the thinnest of threads.

In the midst of this chaos, Eli stood as a beacon of calm. His family, the heart of his world, was being used as a pawn in a game they could not comprehend. The agents' insistence on withholding his children's whereabouts was a tactic born of desperation, a final attempt to control the uncontrollable.

Amanda's anger was a mirror of the world's rage, her voice a clarion call that resonated with the pain of millions. "Was I a trap?" she demanded, her words echoing the betrayal felt by a populace on the brink.

The standoff was a microcosm of the global crisis. Eli, the man who had touched the stars, held the key to salvation or destruction. His next words would tip the balance, for better or for worse.

The standoff in the desert, a stark tableau against the backdrop of a world in disarray, was reaching its zenith. Eli, standing firm amidst the encircling agents, was the eye of the storm—a man whose very presence challenged the reality of those around him.

Amanda's voice, once soft and comforting, was now a clarion call that cut through the tension. "Was I a trap?" she repeated, her accusation hanging heavy in the air. The agents, clad in their suits of authority, shifted uncomfortably, their silence an admission of their tactics.

Eli's gaze was unwavering, his stance that of a man who had faced the unknown and returned with truths that could either mend or shatter the world. "You cannot use my family as leverage," he stated, his voice resonating with a power that seemed to transcend his human form. "I will not be coerced into revealing what must be shared freely."

The agents, sensing the futility of their position, began to relent. "Your children are being brought here," one of them conceded, the words forced out as if against his will. "They will be here within the hour."

The Unraveling

The news was a balm to Amanda's frayed nerves, a promise that the family she had held together through sheer will was about to be reunited. But the relief was short-lived, as the sound of chaos from beyond the perimeter walls filtered through, a reminder of the world teetering on the brink.

Eli turned his attention to the horizon, where plumes of smoke rose from the city streets, the fires of unrest a testament to a civilization at war with itself. The riots, sparked by fear and fueled by uncertainty, were a symptom of a deeper malaise that had taken root in the heart of humanity.

The religious zealots, their fervent cries a soundtrack to the unfolding drama, spoke of judgment and redemption, their words ensnaring the hearts of those who sought answers in the divine. Governments, once the bastions of order, now found themselves impotent, their authority eroded by the tide of events they could neither predict nor control.

Eli knew that the knowledge he possessed was a key that could unlock a future of untold possibilities or seal the fate of a species that had lost its way. The power to heal or to harm lay within the truths he had gleaned from beyond the stars.

As the hour drew near, the sound of approaching vehicles signaled the arrival of Eli's children. The agents, now mere bystanders in a narrative that had outgrown their command, stepped aside as Desirae, Sarah, and

Elijah Junior were escorted through the throng of officials.

The reunion was a moment of pure emotion, a tapestry of tears, laughter, and embraces that spoke of love's enduring strength. Eli held his family close, their presence a reminder of what he had fought for, what he had returned to save.

Chapter 14:

BEYOND THE EVENT HORIZON

The world waited, breathless, as Eli prepared to reveal the truths that would either usher in an era of enlightenment or cast a shadow over the future of all humankind.

In the hallowed halls of the Pentagon, a gathering like no other took place. Religious leaders, world leaders, and presidents sat in a semi-circle, their faces etched with anticipation and fear. At the center of this unprecedented assembly was Eli, a man who had ventured beyond the known universe and returned.

His story began with trepidation. "Two weeks after I lost communication with Earth," Eli recounted, "I was alone, surrounded by an oppressive blackness that stretched into infinity. The Earth was a distant speck of light, my last tether to home."

As he approached the event horizon, the boundary where space and time warped beyond comprehension, Eli braced for the end. The pressure mounted, a physical manifestation of his fear, and then darkness consumed everything.

"But then," Eli continued, his voice steady, "a bright light erupted, blinding and pure." When his vision cleared, the sight that greeted him was beyond imagination. A planet, similar to Earth but twice its size, orbited among several others, each unique and vibrant.

The orbit was alive with activity—space stations and structures that defied earthly architecture. His ship, caught in a tractor beam, was pulled towards this alien world. "I hid," Eli admitted, "fearing what awaited me."

As his ship descended, the panorama of an advanced civilization unfolded before him. Technology that made Earth's finest achievements seem primitive by comparison. And when the ship landed, it was not an alien that greeted him, but a human.

"She was gentle, her smile reassuring," Eli described. "She told me not to be afraid." The confusion was overwhelming. Hundreds of human-like beings surrounded him, their presence a puzzle with no easy solution.

Eli's senses were overwhelmed by the sights and sounds of this new world. The air was filled with the harmonious hum of machinery, seamlessly integrated with the natural environment. The beings that surrounded him moved with a grace and purpose that spoke of a society in perfect sync.

The woman who had greeted him, whom he would come to know as Lira, guided him through the bustling streets. The architecture was a blend of organic curves and crystalline structures, towering spires that seemed to grow from the ground itself. The city was alive, a pulsating heart of a civilization that had transcended the limitations of Earthly existence.

As they walked, Lira explained that their society was built on the principles of unity and the pursuit of knowledge. "We are explorers, seekers of truth," she said. "Our mission is to understand the universe and our place within it."

Eli listened, his mind racing to keep up with the flood of information. He learned of their advancements in energy, medicine, and quantum physics—fields that on Earth were still in their infancy. Here, they were the foundation of everyday life.

The people he passed regarded him with curiosity but not fear. They were a people who had never known war or conflict, whose history was not marred by the struggles that plagued humanity. They greeted him with nods and smiles, welcoming him as one of their own.

Lira led Eli to a central plaza, where a monument stood—a spiraling column of light that reached towards the sky. "This is the Beacon," she said. "It is our connection to the cosmos, a symbol of our journey from the stars."

Eli's gaze followed the column upward, where it seemed to touch the heavens. It was then that he realized the sky was different here. There were two suns, twin orbs that bathed the planet in a perpetual golden twilight.

As the day turned to evening, Eli was brought to a council of the world's leaders. They gathered in a chamber where the walls were adorned with holographic images of galaxies and nebulas, a reminder of the vastness of space.

The council listened intently as Eli shared his story, his journey through the black hole, and his life on Earth. "I come from a world divided," he told them. "A world where fear often outweighs hope, where the pursuit of power overshadows the pursuit of knowledge."

The leaders exchanged thoughtful looks, their expressions a mix of concern and contemplation. "Your world and ours are not so different," one of them spoke. "We too faced such challenges, eons ago. But we chose a different path, one of harmony and enlightenment." One of the leaders began to speak more, but was interrupted. "It is not our place to tell him," One of the leaders intervened. "He is not ready for the truth."

Eli's heart swelled with a mixture of hope, sadness, and confusion. Could Earth ever reach such heights? Was it possible for humanity to overcome its darker nature and embrace a future like this? What truth? What is being hidden from me? He thought.

Eli was emotionally and physically exhausted. He was shown to where he would be staying. A beautiful palace. He entered his room and as soon as he touched the bed his body passed out with exhaustion.

Eli's last memory before succumbing to unconsciousness was the thought that he had returned home, to a dream Earth untouched by the chaos he had left behind.

Chapter 15:
REVELATIONS OF ELOXON 5

Eli's consciousness returned in a room that was the epitome of futuristic elegance. The wall before him was a vast expanse of screen, wrapping around in a panoramic display that blurred the lines between technology and art. As he reached out to touch the digital canvas, a woman entered, her presence as sudden as it was graceful.

"I'm sorry for startling you," she said, guiding him back to the bed with a gentle hand. "Mother will be here soon, and she will answer all your questions."

Later, as the daylight waned, a woman entered, flanked by a male and female, all adorned in garments that shimmered with embedded jewels. This woman, known as Mother, embraced Eli with an affection that was both foreign and familiar. "I have missed you so much, welcome home," she whispered.

Eli, still adrift in a sea of confusion, insisted he had never met her and that this place was not his home. Mother's smile was patient, and she beckoned him to walk with her through the immaculate residence they stood in.

As they strolled, Mother unveiled the history of Eloxon 5. "We are not from Earth, nor are we human as you understand it," she explained. "Our civilization has thrived in peace and harmony for over two millennia."

She spoke of their scientists who, a millennium prior, had discovered a means to traverse galaxies, creating what Earthlings called a black hole, but they named Galgatha. This gateway allowed them to explore distant worlds, with Earth becoming a subject of their attention and, eventually, their concern.

"Humanity's path troubled us," Mother continued. "The species' penchant for destruction, consumption, and violence was heart-wrenching. We felt compelled to intervene, to offer guidance in the hope of altering Earth's self-destructive course."

Eli listened, the tale unfolding like the pages of a book he had never dared to imagine. Mother revealed that they had periodically sent emissaries to Earth, beings of Eloxon 5 who shared their wisdom and genius, hoping to steer humanity towards a brighter future.

"Each attempt ended in tragedy," she lamented. "The people either weaponized our gifts or led our emissaries astray. Among the last we sent were those you know as Albert Einstein, Robert Oppenheimer, and Stephen Hawking."

The revelation struck Eli like a thunderbolt, the implications staggering. The great minds of Earth's history, architects of modern science and thought, were the lost children of Eloxon 5.

Eli grappled with the enormity of Mother's revelations, the walk through the home of Eloxon 5 now a journey through the possibilities of what could have been and what still might be.

Chapter 16:

THE CHOSEN ONE

Eli stood in the midst of Eloxon 5, a world that was both alien and familiar, as Mother continued to unveil the staggering truth of his origin and purpose.

The plan had been set in motion long before Eli's consciousness had grappled with the concept of self. Sent to Earth as an infant, he was to be the silent observer, the hidden guide, and ultimately, the judge of humanity's worthiness to continue its existence.

"The Earth is a rarity in the cosmos," Mother explained, her voice tinged with a reverence for the blue planet that had cradled her son. "Life there teems with a vibrancy that is precious and unique. But its inhabitants have strayed far from the path of harmony."

As the truth settled around him like stardust, Eli found himself grappling with a reality that was both extraordinary and terrifying. Mother's words echoed in his mind, a revelation that reshaped his very existence.

"You are the child of Eloxon 5, sent to Earth to live, learn, and ultimately judge," Mother explained, her voice a mixture of pride and melancholy. "Your life among humans was by design, to grow with them, to become one of them, so that one day you could make an informed decision about their fate."

Eli's mind raced with the memories of Earth—its beauty and its chaos, its capacity for love and its inclination towards destruction. The decision he was to make felt like a burden too immense for any one being to bear.

"Why must it be destruction?" Eli asked, the thought of eradicating the world he knew as home sending a shiver through his spine.

Mother's response was solemn. "It is not a desire for destruction, but a necessity for preservation. If humanity cannot be steered away from its self-destructive tendencies, then the Earth must be given a chance to flourish anew, without the blight of its current custodians."

Eli's heart ached at the thought. To save or to condemn—the choice was his, and his alone. The fate of billions rested upon his judgment, a judgment that would either be a testament to mercy or a sentence of oblivion.

Mother's gaze swept across the horizon of Eloxon 5, her eyes reflecting the verdant landscapes and the harmonious cities that thrived under twin suns. "Our world was not always the haven of peace you see now," she began, her voice a soft echo of times long past. "We once stood where Earth stands today, on the precipice of self-annihilation."

Eli listened intently as Mother recounted the history of Eloxon 5, a tale of a civilization that had teetered on the edge of oblivion. Wars had ravaged the planet, leaving scars that ran deep in the collective memory of its people. Famine and drought had been constant companions, and the air had been thick with the cries of the aggrieved and the oppressed.

"It was a dark epoch," Mother continued, "when rage, hate, and jealousy festered in the hearts of our ancestors. But amidst the chaos, a flicker of hope endured—the hope that we could rise above our basest instincts."

The turning point came, she explained, when a group of visionary scientists and thinkers discovered what they called the Key of Change—a breakthrough that would alter the course of their world forever. This key was not a physical object but a concept, a new way of understanding the interconnectedness of all life and the potential for collective prosperity.

"With the Key of Change, we transformed our society," Mother said, her hands gesturing to the world around them. "Science became our salvation. We eradicated sickness and disease, ensuring that not one of our citizens would know the pain of hunger or the thirst of deprivation."

Eli's eyes widened as he absorbed the magnitude of their achievements. "And aging?" he asked, a question born of his own fear of mortality.

Mother smiled, a hint of pride in her eyes. "We unlocked the secrets of longevity. Our lifespans are now measured in millennia, should we choose it. We live long enough to see the fruits of our labor, to watch our world flourish from generation to generation."

The revelation was staggering. Eli thought of Earth, with its fleeting lives and its relentless struggle against the ravages of time. Could such a future be possible for his home planet? A world where every life is cherished, where every individual has the opportunity to contribute to the greater good?

Eli's gaze lingered on the children below, their laughter a melody that transcended the stars. The vehicles, which hovered gracefully above them, were a testament to Eloxon 5's commitment to the sanctity of life. Here, technology served not as a means to an end, but as an extension of the planet's ethos—a harmony between progress and preservation.

Mother's voice was a gentle guide as she elaborated on the societal structure that sustained their world. "We have no need for military or police as you know them," she explained. "Our society is built on mutual respect and a deep understanding of the consequences of our actions. Disputes are rare, and when they arise, they are resolved through dialogue and empathy, not force."

Eli found the concept both alien and profoundly beautiful. On Earth, conflict was a constant, peace a fleeting dream. Here, peace was the foundation upon which everything else was built.

"The protection we maintain," Mother continued, "is not against our own people but against the unknowns of the universe. Our guardians are watchers, not warriors. They ensure that the peace we've cultivated within is not disturbed by external forces."

As they walked through the city, Eli observed the seamless integration of nature and technology. Buildings were adorned with verdant foliage, their walls alive with plants that purified the air and brought nature into the heart of the metropolis. The energy that powered the city was drawn from the planet's dual suns, a clean and inexhaustible source that fueled their advanced society.

Transportation was a marvel of efficiency and safety. The vehicles, guided by an intricate network of sensors, moved in a ballet of synchronized motion, their paths dictated by algorithms designed to optimize travel and minimize risk.

Eli's attention was drawn to a group of individuals engaged in what appeared to be a public forum. Mother noticed his interest and smiled. "Debate and discussion are encouraged here. Our citizens are active participants in the governance of our world. Decisions are made collectively, with each voice valued and heard."

The economy of Eloxon 5 was another revelation. There was no currency as Eli knew it; instead, the economy was based on resource management and energy credits, a system that ensured every individual's needs were met without the exploitation of others or the planet.

Education was universal and lifelong. Children and adults alike attended learning centers where knowledge was shared freely, and curiosity was the currency of advancement. The pursuit of understanding was not just a right but a cherished duty.

Healthcare was equally revolutionary. Medical centers were hubs of innovation, where the prevention of illness was as important as the cure. The citizens of Eloxon 5 enjoyed robust health, their lifespans a testament to the efficacy of their medical science.

As the tour concluded, Eli stood once more on the balcony, the panorama of Eloxon 5 spread out before him. Mother's hand rested gently on his shoulder. "This is what we offer Earth," she said. "A chance to rewrite its story, to choose a path of unity and longevity, or the path of destruction which will lead to their extermination for the planets sake."

Eli's heart was heavy with the knowledge that Earth's salvation lay within reach. The choice before him was monumental, not just for his own world but for the legacy he would leave behind. Could he be the catalyst for Earth's transformation, or would he witness its downfall from afar?

Chapter 17:
THE MIND'S HORIZON

Eli's days on Eloxon 5 were a blend of wonder and longing. As he immersed himself in the teachings of his newfound home, his heart ached for Earth and the family he had left behind. The revelation of the time differential between the worlds weighed heavily on him; for every 6 months that passed here, a year spun away on Earth.

The population of Eloxon 5 was vast, a testament to the success of their society. To accommodate their numbers and maintain the balance with nature, they had terraformed smaller planets within their system, each a reflection of Eloxon 5's beauty and harmony. These sister worlds, connected by a network of quantum bridges, were a family of civilizations living in unity.

Eli's training began with the fundamentals of their philosophy—**the Unity of Thought and Matter.** His mentors, scholars of the mind's potential, taught him that all matter was interconnected through the fabric of thought, a tapestry that could be altered by the will.

"The energy that binds the universe is the same that powers your thoughts," his mentor, a serene individual named Caelum, explained. "To manipulate the physical, you must first master the mental."

Eli learned to focus his thoughts, to channel the energy of his mind into a tangible force. He started with simple exercises, levitating small objects or bending streams of water with his concentration. The sensation was exhilarating, a feeling of being attuned to the very essence of existence.

As his skills grew, so did the complexity of his tasks. He learned to construct and deconstruct matter, to weave and unweave the threads that held molecules together. He built structures of light and air, only to disperse them back into the nothingness from which they came.

The philosophy of Eloxon 5 was rooted in the belief that all life was sacred, and the power they wielded was never for destruction but for creation and understanding. "With great power comes the responsibility to uphold the sanctity of all existence," Caelum reminded him.

Eli's most challenging lesson was the art of reaching into the minds of others. This ability, revered and feared in equal measure, was the pinnacle of their mental prowess. It required a deep empathy and an unwavering respect for the sanctity of the individual.

He practiced on volunteers, fellow students who guided him through the labyrinth of the mind. He learned to soothe the restless thoughts, to bring peace where there was turmoil. With a gentle touch of his mind, he could lull them into a restful sleep, a skill that mirrored the care with which Eloxon 5 tended to its people.

But it was not just the manipulation of objects or the calming of minds that comprised Eli's training. It was the understanding that this power was an extension of the self, a manifestation of the soul's desire to connect with the universe.

Eli spent hours in meditation, exploring the depths of his consciousness. He discovered reservoirs of strength he never knew he possessed, and with each passing day, his connection to Eloxon 5 deepened.

Yet, even as he marveled at the wonders he could perform, Eli never lost sight of his purpose. He was here to learn, to grow, and to bring back a message of hope to Earth. The knowledge he gained was not for him alone; it was a gift he intended to share with his home planet, a beacon to guide humanity to a brighter future.

Eli's training on Eloxon 5 continued to expand his understanding of their advanced technology and the philosophical underpinnings that shaped their society. One of the most profound abilities he learned was the art of telepathic communication. The Eloxonians had long ago transcended the need for spoken language, their thoughts intermingling with an ease that made verbal exchanges seem archaic.

Caelum, Eli's mentor, guided him through the process of opening his mind to others. "It is about trust," Caelum explained. "To communicate in this way, you must be willing to share a part of yourself with others, to connect on a level that is deeper than words."

Eli practiced with Caelum, learning to lower the mental barriers he had unconsciously erected. At first, the influx of thoughts was overwhelming, a cacophony of voices that threatened to drown out his own. But with time and patience, he learned to filter the noise, to engage in silent conversations that were as clear and nuanced as any spoken dialogue.

The technology of Eloxon 5 facilitated this telepathic link, amplifying and refining the natural abilities of its people. Devices embedded in the environment acted as conduits for thought, ensuring that communication was seamless, whether one was speaking to someone in the same room or across the planet.

Eli found humor in the Eloxonians' reaction to his Earthly habits. Accustomed to holding a phone to his ear, he often found himself mimicking the motion out of habit during telepathic exchanges. The first time he did it, the room erupted in laughter, the Eloxonians finding his quaint gesture endearing.

"It is a reminder of where you come from, Eli," Lira said, her amusement evident in her thoughts. "It is good to remember our roots, even as we embrace new ways."

As Eli's training progressed, he delved deeper into the philosophy that governed Eloxon 5. He attended lectures on the **Ethics of Interconnectivity**, a principle that taught the importance of every action and its ripple effect across the cosmos. The Eloxonians believed that every thought, every deed, was woven into the fabric of reality, and as such, each individual was responsible for the harmony of the whole.

The technology of Eloxon 5 was a physical manifestation of this philosophy. Buildings were equipped with systems that responded to the emotional and physical needs of their inhabitants, adjusting lighting, temperature, and even the structure itself to create an optimal living environment.

Transportation was another marvel of their technological prowess. Vehicles operated on a network of thought, responding to the intentions of their passengers with precision. Accidents were unheard of, as each vehicle was aware of its surroundings and the intentions of others, creating a dance of motion that was both efficient and elegant.

Eli's understanding of Eloxon 5's technology grew, and with it, his appreciation for the delicate balance they had struck between advancement and sustainability. The planet thrived because its people respected the power they wielded, using it not for conquest or control, but for the betterment of all.

Eli marveled at the technological symphony that orchestrated life on Eloxon 5. The dual suns, a pair of celestial guardians, bathed the planet in life-sustaining light, their energy harnessed by colossal Dyson spheres. These structures, feats of engineering genius, captured solar power with near-perfect efficiency, distributing it across the planet and its sister worlds. The energy was the lifeblood of the civilization, fueling every aspect of their advanced society.

The weather, a system once wild and untamed, was now a harmonious ballet under the people's guidance. Advanced climate control technologies allowed the Eloxonians to maintain ideal conditions for their ecosystems. Tornadoes, hurricanes, and other natural disasters were relics of the past, spoken of only in history lessons. Volcanic activity, too, had been quelled by their deep understanding of planetary geology, ensuring that the land remained fertile and safe.

Wildlife roamed freely across the lush landscapes of Eloxon 5, creatures that mirrored the diversity of Earth's fauna yet lived in a peaceful coexistence with the populace. They were not feral but shared a bond with the Eloxonians, a mutual respect that was a cornerstone of the planet's philosophy. The animals thrived, their well-being a priority in a world where all life was cherished.

Agriculture was a testament to the planet's abundance. Fields and orchards stretched as far as the eye could see, yielding bountiful harvests that sustained the vast population. The food was free of chemicals, grown in rich soil and nurtured by the gentle hands of those who revered the act of cultivation. Fast food, a concept so prevalent on Earth, was unheard of here. The Eloxonians dined on meals that were both nourishing and a celebration of nature's gifts.

Health was not maintained through pharmacies or artificial means but through a deep understanding of the body's natural processes. Medical advancements had eradicated the need for synthetic drugs. Instead, healing was achieved through energy manipulation, regenerative therapies, and a diet that kept the population in optimal health. Overweight and obesity, symptoms of Earth's excesses, were non-issues on Eloxon 5.

For those seeking an escape, a respite from the rigors of daily life, the options were as vast as the universe itself. The mind's abilities, honed through training and meditation, allowed one to embark on journeys of the psyche, exploring realms of thought and consciousness that provided rest and rejuvenation.

And for those with a desire to venture beyond the confines of their world, space travel was a common endeavor. The Eloxonians explored the stars not as conquerors but as students, their ships voyaging through the cosmos in a quest for knowledge and connection.

Eli spent hours discussing philosophy and ethics with scholars, learning how the Eloxonians' respect for life extended to all their endeavors. Their technology was not a means of control but a path to enlightenment, a way to elevate their existence and ensure that every individual lived a life of purpose and fulfillment.

Eli's exploration of Eloxon 5's cultural and societal structures took him to places where the past, present, and future of this advanced civilization converged. Museums dedicated to their history were not mere repositories of artifacts; they were interactive experiences that allowed visitors to relive the pivotal moments that shaped their society. Eli walked through exhibits that depicted the transformation from a world on the brink of destruction to one of peace and prosperity. He saw the wars that once ravaged the planet and the subsequent awakening that led to unity and harmony.

The hospitals were temples of healing, where the integration of technology and natural remedies provided care that was both advanced and holistic. Eli observed the birth of new life on Eloxon 5, a process steeped in both science and tradition. Here, the act of giving birth was entrusted to designated Mothers—women who had dedicated their lives to nurturing the next generation. These Mothers were revered, their role seen as both a duty and an honor.

Eli learned that his own birth mother had brought forth 2,000 children into the world, a staggering number by Earth's standards. Among them were his companions, the male named Zandur and female Soloice who had been at his side since his return, and the caretaker of his home. The palace he resided in, a structure of elegance and tranquility, had been crafted specifically for him, a symbol of his unique place in their world.

Yet, despite the beauty and serenity that surrounded him, Eli couldn't help but feel a pang of sorrow for the mothers. Theirs was a life of service, devoid of the emotional bonds that he associated with parenthood. They bore children with a sense of duty, not of love, their hearts insulated from the joys and pains of maternal affection.

The exception was his own mother, who defied the norm. Her love for her children was palpable, a warmth that radiated from her being. She had raised Eli's siblings with a tenderness that belied the clinical nature of their society's approach to childbirth.

When a child was born, they were placed in the care of the genetic parents, the ones who had contributed their DNA to the creation of new life. Yet, all children, regardless of their upbringing, referred to the mothers with the same reverence and respect, acknowledging the vital role they played in the continuation of their species.

Eli's days were filled with learning and reflection. He grappled with the complexities of Eloxon 5's approach to life, the balance they struck between emotion and duty, love and responsibility. The planet's peaceful facade belied the depth of thought and the weight of decisions that had forged such a society.

As he lay in his bed at night, staring up at the stars that were both familiar and foreign, Eli pondered the lessons he could take back to Earth. Could his home planet adopt the philosophies of Eloxon 5? Was it possible for humanity to redefine its understanding of love, duty, and parenthood in a way that would lead to a brighter future?

Chapter 18:

THE RETURN AND THE REVELATION

After a decade of profound growth and learning on Eloxon 5, Eli Jacobson was ready to embark on his return journey to Earth. The planet had become a second home to him, a utopia free from malice, where the concept of evil seemed as alien as he once was. The absence of malevolence on Eloxon 5 was a stark contrast to the Earth he remembered, and it left Eli with a sense of wonder and a sliver of doubt. Could such a world truly exist, or was he viewing it through the rose-colored lens of hope?

His ship, now a familiar haven, had been upgraded with the pinnacle of Eloxonian technology. It was designed not only for comfort but also for seamless travel between the stars, ensuring that Eli could return to Eloxon 5 at will. The thought of being able to traverse the vastness of space with such ease brought Eli a sense of freedom he had never known.

Accompanying him on his journey were his siblings, Zandur and Soloice, who had been constant companions during his time on Eloxon 5. Their presence was a comfort, their kindness a balm to the apprehension that gnawed at him. The Elders had warned Eli that Earth might not welcome him back with open arms. He would be seen as an outsider, a potential threat harboring knowledge that could either save or doom humanity.

Eli's ship was now equipped with a force field, invisible yet impenetrable, capable of expanding to protect an entire state if necessary. This dome of safety was a microcosm of Eloxon 5, impervious to external forces and controlled solely by Eli's will. It was a sanctuary that he could extend to others, a shield against the chaos he feared he would find on Earth.

As the day of departure dawned, Eli, Zandur, and Soloice boarded the ship, their hearts heavy with the weight of their mission. Eli's excitement to see his family again was tempered by the knowledge of what his return might entail. The Elders' warnings echoed in his mind, a foreboding prelude to the challenges that lay ahead.

The journey through space was a silent ascent into the unknown. The black hole, a gateway between worlds, loomed before them, a swirling maelstrom of darkness and light. Eli's hand hovered over the controls, his resolve firm. He initiated the sequence that would open the portal back to Earth, his thoughts on the loved ones he yearned to see.

In the moments before the ship entered the black hole, Eli cast a final glance back at Eloxon 5. The planet's beauty was a vision that would forever be etched in his memory. But something new caught his eye—a colossal ship stationed on the far side of the planet. It was unlike any vessel he had seen during his time on Eloxon 5, resembling a military behemoth from Earth's oceans.

A sense of unease washed over Eli. The presence of such a ship in this peaceful world was an anomaly that he could not ignore. It stood in stark contrast to everything he had learned about Eloxon 5, a shadow on the horizon of his departure.

As the ship entered the black hole, the image of the mysterious vessel faded from view, replaced by the kaleidoscope of colors that danced at the edge of reality. Eli's last thoughts of Eloxon 5 were a mix of gratitude and concern, the joy of his time there now tinged with the specter of a threat he could not understand.

As Eli's ship pierced the event horizon of the black hole, a sense of calm enveloped him. The familiar pull of the void, which had once filled him with dread, now brought a thrill of anticipation. The ship, a vessel of Eloxonian ingenuity, hummed with energy, its systems responding to the tumultuous forces outside with grace and precision.

The sights that unfolded before Eli and his siblings, Zandur and Soloice, were a cosmic ballet of light and darkness. Streams of stellar dust and gas spiraled around them, painting the void with swathes of iridescent color. The stars, distant and serene, watched silently as the ship navigated the currents of space-time.

Eli, now a seasoned traveler of the cosmos, took in the spectacle with a sense of awe. He understood the mechanics of what he was witnessing—the bending of light, the stretching of space—but the beauty of it transcended knowledge. It was a reminder of the vastness of the universe and the smallness of his own existence within it.

Zandur and Soloice sat quietly, their eyes wide with wonder. They had been born and raised on Eloxon 5, a world without night, and the sight of the infinite stars' cape was new to them. Eli watched their faces, illuminated by the celestial light show, and felt a surge of protectiveness. They were far from home, and he was responsible for their safety.

As the ship emerged from the black hole, the blue marble of Earth came into view. It was a poignant moment for Eli, a homecoming that stirred a tumult of emotions within him. He gazed at the planet, its continents and oceans a tapestry of life, and felt both joy and trepidation.

For days, they orbited Earth, Eli deep in thought as he planned their approach. He knew the world he was returning to was not the one he had left. Fear and suspicion had likely grown in his absence, and the knowledge he carried was both a gift and a burden.

Eli instructed Zandur and Soloice to remain hidden within the ship once they landed. "The people of Earth may not understand who you are," he warned them. "They may see you as a threat. It's imperative that you stay out of sight until I can ensure your safety."

His siblings nodded, their trust in Eli absolute. They understood the gravity of the situation and the potential danger they faced. The ship's force field would be their sanctuary, an invisible shield against the chaos of Earth.

Eli's thoughts were a whirlwind as he considered his next steps. How would he be received? Would the government listen to what he had to say, or would they see him as an enemy? The thought of being separated from his family again, of being treated as a hostile force, was a sharp pain in his heart.

Yet, amidst the fear, there was a burning desire to see Amanda and his children. He longed to hold them, to tell them of his journey and the wonders he had seen. The thought of their embrace gave him the strength to face the uncertainty that awaited him.

The descent through Earth's atmosphere was a silent ballet of fire and precision. Eli's ship, a gleaming testament to Eloxonian technology, cut through the sky, its force field shimmering against the heat of re-entry. Below, the vast expanse of the desert awaited, an ocean of sand and solitude that would serve as the cradle for their return.

As the ship touched down, a cloud of dust billowed around them, the only witness to their arrival the barren landscape and the stars above. Eli, Zandur, and Soloice remained within the safety of the vessel, the silence of the desert a stark contrast to the cacophony of messages that began to flood their communication systems.

The military, ever vigilant, had not missed the arrival of the unidentified craft. Messages of warning, demands for identification, and thinly-veiled threats poured in, a relentless stream of paranoia and fear. Eli listened, his expression one of sadness and resolve. He understood their fear, the instinct to defend against the unknown, but it pained him to be received with hostility rather than hope.

From the ship's monitors, Eli and his siblings watched the world outside. Military vehicles converged on the landing site, their movements precise and calculated. Soldiers established a perimeter, their weapons trained on the silent ship that had appeared so unexpectedly in their midst.

The state of the world was as he had feared. The news feeds told stories of governments in turmoil, societies grappling with uncertainty, and a people divided. The Earth he had left behind was now a planet on the edge, its future hanging in the balance.

The Return and the Revelation

For two days, they watched and waited. Eli's heart ached for his family, for the reunion that was so close yet felt worlds away. He longed to step outside, to feel the sun on his face and the wind in his hair, to embrace his wife and children. But he knew that the world outside was not ready for what he and his siblings represented.

Zandur and Soloice, ever patient, trusted in Eli's wisdom. They had seen the beauty of Earth from afar, but now they witnessed its chaos, a chaos that mirrored the past of their own world before the awakening that had led to peace.

As the sun set on the second day, Eli gathered his siblings. "Remember the plan," he reminded them, his voice firm. "You must stay within the ship. The force field will protect you, and the technology within will sustain you. I must face them alone."

Zandur and Soloice nodded, their faces a mixture of concern and courage. "We will be here, waiting for your return," Soloice said, her voice a gentle melody in the quiet of the ship.

Eli placed his hand on the console, the ship responding to his touch. The ramp lowered, and he stepped out into the twilight of the desert, the force field retracting behind him to shield the ship from view.

Chapter 19:
THE VEIL OF INTENTIONS

---※---

Eli Jacobson stood in the center of the grand hall, the weight of the world's gaze upon him. Cameras captured his every word, broadcasting his extraordinary tale to every corner of the planet. The story of Eloxon 5, his journey through the black hole, and the advanced civilization that had become his second home was now the collective narrative of Earth.

The room, filled with government officials and world leaders, was thick with intrigue. The President of the United States leaned forward, his question piercing the charged atmosphere. "Is everything you've told us true, Mr. Jacobson?" he asked, the gravity of the situation evident in his tone.

Eli's affirmation was firm, his voice resonating with the truth of his experiences. "Yes, Mr. President. Every word," he replied, locking eyes with the leader of the free world.

A murmur rippled through the assembly as generals and advisors excused themselves, retreating to a private chamber to deliberate the implications of Eli's revelations. Left in the hall with his family, Eli's extraordinary senses extended beyond the walls that separated them from the clandestine meeting.

The voices of the world's most powerful individuals were clear in his mind, their intentions laid bare. Discussions of commandeering his ship, of exploiting the technology of Eloxon 5 for Earth's gain, filled the room. Some spoke of opportunity, of the advancements that could be made; others spoke of fear, of the need to neutralize a potential threat.

Eli's heart sank as he listened to the plotting, the plans to dissect his knowledge, to dissect him. The leaders' words were a dark echo of the warnings given by the Elders of Eloxon 5. They had foreseen this greed, this hunger for power that had so often led humanity astray.

As he stood there, surrounded by his family yet isolated by the truth, Eli grappled with the enormity of his situation. The leaders of Earth saw Eloxon 5 not as a beacon of hope, but as a resource to be plundered. The parallels between Earth's tumultuous history and the past of Eloxon 5 were stark, a cycle of conquest and destruction that Eli had hoped was behind them.

Eli's thoughts were a storm, his resolve tested by the whispers of betrayal. He remembered the peace of Eloxon 5, the harmony that resonated through every aspect of life there. The thought of Earth's leaders bringing their chaos to that serene world was unbearable.

He turned to his family, their faces a mix of confusion and concern. Amanda's eyes met his, a silent question within them. Eli's expression was one of determination, a silent promise that he would protect both his worlds.

Eli closes his eyes and remembers reaffirming the plan to his siblings, Zandur and Soloice. "Stay hidden, stay safe," he instructed, his voice a low command. "Trust in me, as I trust in you. We will not let the darkness of fear overshadow the light of our knowledge."

As the generals returned, their faces masks of diplomacy, Eli prepared himself for the confrontation to come. He was the bridge between two worlds, and he would not let the short-sighted desires of a few dictates the fate of many.

Eli Jacobson, once a man of Earth, now stood as its potential savior or its harbinger of doom. The path ahead was fraught with peril, but Eli knew that the future was not written in the stars—it was written in the hearts and minds of those who dared to dream of a better tomorrow.

The grand hall, once a place of diplomacy and discussion, had transformed into a theater of conflict. The world leaders, having dismissed the media in a bid to cloak their actions from public view, now faced the consequences of their decisions broadcasted for all to see.

The President of the United States, his voice laden with authority, had demanded Eli's compliance. "As a citizen, you are duty-bound to obey," he declared, his order for Eli to surrender his ship echoing off the walls. But Eli, standing resolute, did not waver. His stance was unyielding, a testament to his conviction and the truth he carried.

The tension in the room was palpable as the other officials and leaders observed the standoff. The President's assertion that Eli could not face the world alone was a veiled threat, an attempt to coerce him into submission. Yet, Eli's gaze did not falter; it was clear and determined.

Amanda, sensing the rising danger, acted swiftly, guiding Elijah Jr. and the others out of the room. Eli's warning to the assembly was a stark reminder of their impotence in the face of true power. "You cannot control what is to come," he cautioned. "The leaders of this world are the problem. I will offer the people a chance to save it."

As Eli gestured behind the President, the officials turned to witness the impossible—a news camera, suspended in mid-air, recording every moment. The realization that their actions were being transmitted live, for the world to judge, sent a ripple of panic through the room.

The response was immediate and violent. Guns were drawn, military personnel flooded the room, and the air was filled with the sound of gunfire. The President and other leaders retreated, watching from a distance, hoping against hope that Eli would fall.

But as the smoke cleared, the soldiers were met with a sight that defied belief. Eli stood unharmed, the bullets that had been meant to end his life now lay at his feet, harmless and defeated. The confusion among the ranks was palpable as they scrambled to reload, their eyes fixed on the man who had become an enigma.

Eli watched them with a calm that belied the chaos around him. The camera continued to broadcast, capturing the unfolding drama for the world to witness. As the soldiers took aim once more, their movements halted, frozen in time. One by one, their weapons clattered to the ground, and they slumped to the floor, their consciousness slipping away.

The security detail, desperate to regain control, emerged with flashbangs in hand. But their efforts were futile. The grenades hung suspended in the air, and with a flick of Eli's will, they were propelled back towards the men who had thrown them. The explosions were blinding, the screams of the guards a cacophony of pain and fear.

In the aftermath of the confrontation, the grand hall was a scene of disarray. The air was thick with the residue of conflict, and the ground was littered with the inert forms of soldiers and security personnel. Eli stood amidst the chaos, a solitary figure of calm in the eye of the storm.

The world leaders, who had sought refuge at the first sign of violence, peeked out from their sanctuary, their eyes wide with disbelief. The man they had sought to control, to manipulate for their own ends, had demonstrated powers that defied their understanding of the world.

Eli's family, safely escorted from the room before the conflict erupted, watched from a distance, their faith in Eli unshaken. Amanda's eyes held a mixture of pride and concern, knowing the man she loved was fighting a battle on a scale few could comprehend.

As the dust settled, the camera that Eli had commandeered continued to broadcast live to the world. Every eye on the planet was fixed on the feed, witnessing the extraordinary events that unfolded in the heart of power. The leaders' true intentions, their willingness to resort to violence, were laid bare for all to see.

Eli's voice broke the silence, his words reaching out to the global audience. "People of Earth," he began, his tone imbued with the gravity of the moment, "you have seen the lengths to which your leaders will go to maintain their grip on power. But the future I offer is not one of control and fear. It is a future of understanding, of unity, and of peace."

The camera panned to show the incapacitated soldiers, the evidence of Eli's abilities clear and undeniable. "I do not wish to harm," Eli continued, "but I will protect myself and the knowledge I carry. The choice is yours. Will you follow the path of your leaders, or will you choose a different way?"

As the broadcast ended, the world was left in a state of reflection. The revelation of their leaders' actions and Eli's message of hope sparked a global conversation. The path forward was uncertain, but the possibility of change had been ignited in the hearts of the people.

Chapter 20:
THE GENESIS OF UTOPIA

---※---

Eli Jacobson, with his family in tow, approached the ship that stood as a silent sentinel in the midst of the desert. His siblings, Zandur and Soloice, had instinctively begun to prepare the vessel for departure, their actions driven by the belief that Eli intended to return to Eloxon 5. But Eli's voice, firm yet gentle, halted their preparations. "Power down the ship," he instructed, his command stirring a cloud of confusion that mirrored the dust of the desert.

The siblings complied, their eyes seeking answers in Eli's determined gaze. "We are not leaving," Eli revealed, his words painting a picture of a future that was about to unfold. "I will expand the dome to encompass this entire desert." The siblings exchanged glances, their minds grappling with the magnitude of Eli's vision.

With a thought, Eli commanded the dome to expand, its boundaries stretching outwards until the entire desert was enveloped. The dome solidified, becoming an opaque sphere that shielded its interior from prying eyes. It was a world within a world, accessible only to those whom Eli deemed worthy.

Inside the dome, a transformation began. Grass, green and vibrant, sprouted from the barren sands, covering the desert with a blanket of life. The technology of Eloxon 5, a gift that Eli had brought with him, reshaped the landscape, turning desolation into paradise. Trees took root, flowers bloomed, and streams of crystal-clear water carved through the newly formed terrain.

The dome, a marvel that defied explanation, became the story that spread like wildfire across the globe. People from all corners of the Earth watched, their eyes wide with wonder and their hearts filled with questions. What was this anomaly in the desert? Was it the harbinger of a new age?

Eli, standing at the heart of his creation, reached out with his mind, his message resonating in the consciousness of every human being. "Come to the dome," he beckoned. "Here, I am building a utopia, a sanctuary from the turmoil of your world."

The weather within the dome was a symphony conducted by Eli's will. The sun shone with a gentle warmth, the breeze whispered promises of peace, and the rain fell only to nourish. It was a replica of Eloxon 5, a testament to the harmony that could exist between nature and technology.

The Genesis of Utopia

Eli's proclamation was a siren call to the weary, the oppressed, and the hopeful. "I will come for you," he promised. "In this place, you will be free from the evils that have shadowed your lives. Here, you will find healing for your ailments, solace for your souls, and a chance to begin anew."

Eli and his family exited the ship to see what had been created. Amanda stared in wonder at what she saw. The red desert sand replaced by beautiful green; the scorching temperature replaced with a mild beautiful breeze.

As he turned towards his ship a large section of it suddenly came apart and began floating in the air. It was shaped like a smaller version of the ship. With his mind Eli made two more smaller ships. All the ships were automated drones whose sole purpose was to seek out the chosen and bring them to the dome.

The world watched as Eli's ships, now vessels of salvation, prepared to traverse the skies. They would seek out those who yearned for a better life, who dreamed of a world where health was a birthright and longevity a gift freely given.

Eli, with the help of Zandur and Soloice, set about crafting the foundations of the new world within the dome. With a mere thought, structures began to rise from the once barren desert—homes that blended the beauty of Eloxonian architecture with the familiarity of Earth's designs. The houses were constructed with materials that were both durable and harmonious with the environment, their walls infused with the living energy of the planet.

The siblings worked in unison, their movements a dance of creation. Gardens flourished, filled with flora from both worlds, and fountains sprung up, casting rainbows into the air with their mist. Community centers, libraries, and places of learning took shape, each a hub of future knowledge sharing and cultural exchange.

As they labored, Eli noticed a silent exchange between Zandur and Soloice—a glance that carried a weight he could not decipher. It was a momentary flicker of something concealed, a secret held between them. He felt a twinge of unease, something was amiss, yet, he chose to focus on the task at hand, pushing the feeling to the back of his mind. The urgency of building a sanctuary for humanity overshadowed his personal misgivings.

The utopia they were creating was a beacon of hope. Eli envisioned a society where every individual would have a place to call home, where hunger and illness would be words relegated to history. He imagined children playing in the streets, their laughter a testament to the peace and safety that enveloped them.

But the sense of foreboding lingered, a shadow at the edge of Eli's consciousness. Zandur and Soloice shared a bond beyond his understanding, a connection to their home planet that Eli, raised on Earth, could not fully grasp. They were loyal, of that he had no doubt, but loyalty to whom—or what—remained unclear.

As the sun dipped below the horizon, casting a golden glow over the newly formed landscape, Eli stood at the center of the utopia, his heart swelling with pride and hope. The dome, a microcosm of Eloxon 5's harmony, was his gift to Earth. A chance for humanity to embrace a new way of life.

Within the dome, a new world was taking shape, a testament to the harmony and balance that defined Eloxon 5. Eli, Zandur, and Soloice worked tirelessly, their efforts weaving the fabric of a society that would soon welcome Earth's denizens.

The houses that rose from the Eloxonian soil were marvels of architectural ingenuity, each structure a blend of aesthetic beauty and functional design. They were homes that required no maintenance, their materials self-healing and adaptive to the needs of their inhabitants. The buildings were more than mere shelters; they were living spaces that breathed with the life of the planet, a symbiosis of human need and environmental consciousness.

Gardens flourished under Eli's careful guidance, a mosaic of greenery that sprawled across the landscape. The plants, brought from Eloxon 5, thrived in the rich soil that needed no pesticides, no herbicides—there were no pests to ward off, no weeds to uproot. The flora of Eloxon 5 was resilient and self-sustaining, a perfect complement to the new ecosystem Eli was creating.

Fruits hung heavy on the branches, their flesh sweet and nourishing, free from the taint of chemicals. Vegetables grew in abundance, their colors a vibrant palette against the green backdrop. The gardens were a source of sustenance and a place of tranquility, where future residents could wander and find peace among the whispering leaves.

The grass, a lush carpet beneath their feet, required no cutting. It grew to a perfect height and then sustained itself, a perpetual verdure that invited bare feet and picnics under the open sky. The soil, rich and fertile, needed no tilling. It was a living entity, a part of the greater whole that was Eloxon 5's gift to Earth.

Eli's vision was coming to life, a utopia where harmony was not an ideal but a reality. The dome was a sanctuary, a refuge from the storms that raged beyond its borders. Here, the air was always fresh, the temperature perfect. Rain fell gently, summoned by Eli's will, to water the gardens and fill the streams that meandered through the landscape.

The technology that powered this paradise was invisible, integrated seamlessly into the environment. Energy flowed from the dual suns of Eloxon 5, and shared through technology and the Eloxonians, captured by the dome's surface and distributed with silent efficiency. It powered the homes, the streetlights, and the public spaces, a clean and endless supply that ensured the dome's inhabitants would never want for power.

As the day of opening the dome to Earth's people drew near, Eli watched the horizon with a sense of accomplishment and anticipation. The utopia he had built was a beacon of hope, a promise of what could be achieved when one embraced the potential for change.

Soon, the dome would open its gates, and the first of Earth's citizens would step into a new life, a life free from the shadows of their past. Eli's utopia was ready to become their home, and he was ready to welcome them with open arms.

Chapter 21:
THE WORLD'S CROSSROADS

The world had witnessed a spectacle that would forever alter the course of history. From the conflict within the government building to Eli's powerful display of defiance and the subsequent revelation of the Dome, humanity was left in a state of shock, awe, and introspection.

In homes, cafes, and public squares, people gathered around screens, watching replays of the events, dissecting every moment. The image of Eli, standing unscathed amidst a hail of bullets, had become an icon of resistance against the oppressive forces of the world. His message, a call to join him in a utopia free from the evils that had long plagued society, resonated with the masses.

Tired of the corruption, the wars, and the endless cycle of poverty and despair, people began to mobilize. They packed their belongings, whispered plans in hushed tones, and set their sights on the Dome. It was a pilgrimage, a mass exodus driven by the hope of a better life.

Governments, reeling from the exposure of their true natures, scrambled to regain control. Law enforcement and military personnel were dispatched to key locations, roadblocks erected, and travel restrictions imposed. The leaders of the world, their authority shaken, were desperate to stem the tide of people yearning for Eli's promised sanctuary.

But the human spirit, when ignited by the flame of hope, is not easily quelled. Families slipped through the cracks, individuals vanished into the night, all making their way toward the Dome. It was a movement that no government could stop—a testament to the collective desire for change.

Meanwhile, the governments plotted. In secure facilities, away from the prying eyes of the public, they gathered their top minds—scientists, strategists, and thinkers—to analyze the situation. The Dome, an enigma of technology and power, was a challenge to their supremacy, a threat to the status quo.

They poured over satellite imagery, intercepted communications, and analyzed every piece of data they could glean. Ideas were proposed, from brute force assaults to sophisticated hacking attempts. The goal was singular: to breach the Dome and claim the secrets of Eloxon 5 for themselves.

The World's Crossroads

The discussions were heated, the atmosphere charged with urgency. Some argued for caution, wary of provoking Eli further. Others advocated for aggressive action, fearing the implications of a world divided by the existence of the Dome.

As the days passed, the tension grew. The Dome stood silent in the desert, a beacon of hope for the people and a symbol of defiance against the governments. Inside, Eli and his siblings watched the world's reaction, their hearts heavy with the knowledge of the impending confrontation.

Eli's thoughts were a whirlwind of strategy and concern. He knew the governments would not sit idly by while their citizens flocked to his utopia. The Dome was impregnable, but the people journeying toward it were vulnerable. He had to act, and soon.

Eli's mind raced as he considered the plight of those making the perilous journey to the Dome. He knew that the governments of the world, in their desperation to maintain control, would not hesitate to use force to stop the exodus. The Dome itself might be an unassailable fortress, but its potential inhabitants were still exposed to the dangers of a world not yet ready to embrace change.

The images of families braving checkpoints, of old and young alike traversing treacherous paths, were broadcast across the globe, igniting a fire of solidarity among the people. They saw in Eli's utopia a chance for redemption, a new beginning free from the shackles of a society that had long forgotten the meaning of unity and peace.

But with each passing hour, the situation grew more dire. Reports of clashes between the migrants and military forces began to surface, each confrontation a stark reminder of the divide between the powers that be and the will of the people.

Eli convened a meeting within the Dome, gathering his siblings. They discussed strategies, ways to protect the people from the aggression of the governments, and how to ensure the safe passage of every soul seeking refuge within the Dome.

"We must extend our protection beyond these walls," Eli declared, his voice resolute. "The technology of Eloxon 5 has given us the means to create a sanctuary, but it is our duty to safeguard the path to this haven."

Plans were drawn up, a network of safe routes mapped out, and a system of communication established to guide the people to the Dome. Eli's siblings, Zandur and Soloice, volunteered to act as emissaries, to go out into the world and lead the people home.

As the first of the convoys set out, a sense of hope permeated the air. The Dome's force field expanded, creating a corridor of safety that stretched out into the desert, a beacon for all those who sought a new life.

The world's leaders, watching from their halls of power, were taken aback by the resilience of the people. Their attempts to quell the movement had only served to strengthen it, to unite the people in a common cause that transcended borders and ideologies.

The governments' top minds, gathered in secret, continued to deliberate on how to breach the Dome. They proposed elaborate schemes, from tunneling beneath the force field to launching aerial assaults. Yet, for all their plotting, they could not find a weakness in Eli's creation.

Eli, from within the safety of the Dome, watched the machinations of the world's governments with a heavy heart. His extraordinary abilities allowed him to see and hear their clandestine meetings, their desperate plans to penetrate the sanctuary he had created. The leaders of Earth, driven by fear and greed, were blind to the utopia that thrived mere miles from their grasp.

The schemes they concocted were as varied as they were futile. Engineers and military experts gathered around tables laden with blueprints and models, proposing to tunnel beneath the impenetrable force field or to rain down fire from the skies. Yet, for all their ingenuity, they found no flaw in the Dome's defenses. It was a fortress of peace, impervious to the violence that sought to claim it.

Eli's connection to the Dome was more than technological; it was an extension of his very being. He could sense the vibrations of the Earth beneath it, the air that caressed its surface, and the intentions of those who circled it like wolves at the door. The Dome was a manifestation of his will, a testament to the knowledge of Eloxon 5, and it would not yield to the forces of conquest.

Despite the clarity of the threat, Eli held onto hope. Hope that the leaders would see reason, that they would understand the futility of their aggression. He hoped that the sight of families finding solace within the Dome, of children playing in its meadows, and of the sick being healed by its technology would soften their hearts.

Eli's siblings, Zandur and Soloice, shared in his vigil, their eyes often meeting in silent conversation. They too had heard the plans of the governments, their telepathic abilities picking up the whispers of war. Together, they stood ready to protect the utopia they had helped to build, to shield the people who had placed their trust in Eli's vision.

As the days passed, the stream of people seeking refuge within the Dome grew. They came from all corners of the Earth, braving the obstacles that lay in their path. Eli watched over them, his heart swelling with each new arrival. The Dome was becoming a beacon of hope, a symbol of what humanity could achieve when united by a common purpose.

The utopia finished now, Eli standing atop the highest tower within the Dome, watching the horizon as a line of lights approached—a caravan of the first citizens of the new world. His heart swelled with pride and determination. The Genesis of Utopia was not just a dream; it was becoming a reality.

Chapter 22:
THE THRESHOLD OF INTENT

The arrival of the first group at the Dome marked a pivotal moment in Eli's mission. The caravan, a microcosm of humanity, carried with it the hopes and ailments of a world in turmoil. Eli's heart ached for those lost along the way, casualties of a system that fought against the very hope he offered.

As the Dome's entrance materialized before the weary travelers, it was a gateway to a new beginning. The children, embodiments of innocence and potential, passed through without hindrance, their laughter a balm to Eli's soul. But when the barrier repelled one of their own, confusion rippled through the crowd.

Eli, equally bewildered, was summoned by his siblings, Zandur and Soloice, who shared a glance that spoke volumes. They revealed to him a truth that shook the very foundation of his understanding—the Key of

Eloxon 5, an ethereal judge woven into the fabric of their technology.

This Key, an arbiter of intent, was designed to safeguard the utopia of Eloxon 5 by discerning the nature of its people. It was a guardian that ensured the purity of their society, a silent sentinel that protected the collective from the corruption of the individual.

Eli's shock was palpable as he learned of the Key's function. On Eloxon 5, newborns were gently placed within a basinet shielded by the Dome, where the Key assessed their essence. Those deemed a threat to the harmony of the world were not permitted to exist—a concept that challenged Eli's Earth-born sensibilities.

"Destroyed?" Eli echoed, his voice a mix of horror and disbelief. "How can such a decision be made? By what right does this Key determine the value of a life?"

The siblings explained that the Key was not a tool of malice but of preservation. It was the cornerstone upon which their peaceful society was built, a necessary measure to prevent the rise of evil that once threatened to consume them.

"And now, the Key has come to Earth," they continued, their voices a harmony of solemnity and regret. "Not all who wish to enter the Dome will be allowed. The Key will discern their intentions, past, present, and future. It is the way of Eloxon 5, and now, it must be the way of the Dome."

The Threshold of Intent

Eli grappled with the revelation. The Dome, his gift to humanity, was now a crucible where the worthiness of each soul would be measured. The thought that some would be turned away, that families could be torn apart by an invisible judge, was a bitter pill to swallow.

As the day waned, more travelers arrived, their eyes filled with a mixture of hope and trepidation. Eli watched as they approached the threshold, each one tested by the Key. Most passed through, their spirits lifted by the promise of a new life. But for some, the barrier remained firm, an unyielding wall that denied them entry.

The sun dipped below the horizon, casting long shadows across the faces of those gathered at the Dome's entrance. Eli stood, a silent sentinel, his heart heavy with the knowledge of the Key's judgment. The air was thick with anticipation and the faintest hint of sorrow for those who had been turned away.

As night fell, a somber mood settled over the crowd. Families huddled together, grateful for their acceptance into the Dome, yet their joy was tempered by the sight of those denied entry. Eli watched the rejected with empathy, their confusion and pain a mirror to his own turmoil.

The Key, an arbiter from Eloxon 5, had become the gatekeeper of this new world. It was an impartial judge, its decisions based on criteria that transcended human understanding. Eli knew that the Key's purpose was to ensure the purity and safety of the utopia he had created, but the cost of such security was a burden he had not anticipated.

Eli's siblings, Zandur and Soloice, stood by his side, their expressions solemn. They too felt the weight of the Key's decisions, the responsibility of their heritage casting a long shadow over the promise of the Dome.

As the last of the day's travelers entered the sanctuary, Eli addressed the crowd. "We have embarked on a journey together," he said, his voice carrying across the expanse. "A journey towards a future where peace and harmony reign. But we must also face the reality of the Key's judgment. It is not a punishment, but a safeguard for the world we are building."

Inside the Dome, the transformation was complete. The desert had given way to a verdant paradise, a living testament to the potential of Eloxon 5's technology. Houses stood ready to welcome their new inhabitants, gardens awaited the tender care of those who would cultivate them, and streams flowed with the promise of life.

Eli's message of hope and unity spread beyond the Dome, reaching the ears of those still fighting to reach its gates. It was a call to action, a plea for understanding and compassion in a world that had known too much division.

As the dawn of a new day broke over the Dome, Eli initiated the launch of small drone ships, each one a silent messenger of hope. They soared into the sky, fanning out across the Earth to seek out those who yearned for the sanctuary of the Dome. The drones were equipped with the same technology that protected the Dome, ensuring the safety and comfort of their passengers on the journey back.

Meanwhile, at the entrance of the Dome, a confrontation was brewing. A group of military personnel, disguised as refugees, approached the threshold, their intentions cloaked in deceit. But the Key, ever vigilant, recognized the malice in their hearts and alerted Eli and his siblings through their telepathic link.

Eli, Zandur, and Soloice hastened to the entrance, their expressions set in determination. As the soldiers reached the invisible barrier, they found themselves unable to move forward, the Key's judgment rendered in real-time. Eli approached the immobilized men, his siblings flanking him, their presence a warning to those who would threaten the peace of the Dome.

With a mere thought, Eli and his siblings reached into the minds of the soldiers, their abilities putting the intruders into a deep slumber. Gently, they carried the unconscious men to a secure location within the Dome, away from the prying eyes of the world.

In the quiet of the secured room, Eli delved into the soldiers' minds, extracting the information they held. He saw the plans laid out by their superiors, the strategies devised to infiltrate and claim the Dome. The knowledge was a tapestry of fear and ambition, a plan born from the desperation of a world not ready to let go of its old ways.

The soldiers, upon awakening, found themselves facing Eli and his siblings once more. "You have been given a choice," Eli told them, his voice echoing with the authority of one who had seen beyond the stars. "Return to your leaders with a message: the Dome will not be breached. Any further aggression will be met with consequences that none of you wish to face."

The soldiers, their memories of the encounter wiped clean except for Eli's warning, were escorted to the edge of the Dome and released. They stumbled back into the world, a sense of unease their only companion.

Chapter 23:

A NEW DAWN WITHIN THE DOME

As the first rays of sunlight filtered through the Dome, casting a warm glow over the lush landscape, the new inhabitants began their journey into a world unlike any they had known. The entrance to the Dome, a gateway of light and hope, welcomed them with open arms, each person stepping through with a mix of trepidation and wonder.

The Key, an ethereal guardian of the threshold, hummed softly as it scanned each entrant. It was a silent judge, assessing the hearts and intentions of those who sought refuge within the Dome. For most, the passage was smooth, a seamless transition from the chaos of the outside world to the serenity within.

Once inside, the newcomers were guided to the medical facilities, where Eloxonian technology awaited to mend their ailments. The clinics, staffed by both human and Eloxonian healers, were a marvel of science and compassion. Nanotechnology worked in harmony with advanced medical techniques to restore health and vitality.

Bones, once broken, were healed within minutes, the nanobots weaving new tissue with precision and care. Cancer, a scourge that had claimed so many on Earth, met its match in the chambers designed to seek and destroy malignant cells without harming the healthy ones. Those who had been bound to wheelchairs stood and walked, their paralysis undone by the regenerative powers of Eloxonian medicine. Eyes that had seen the world through a blur found clarity, and diseases like diabetes became a memory, their hold on the body released forever.

The homes that awaited the inhabitants were a testament to the adaptability of Eloxonian architecture. Each dwelling was a living entity, responsive to the needs of its occupants. Families, large and small, found spaces that accommodated them perfectly. When an extra bedroom was needed, the house would shift, walls moving with a quiet grace to create new spaces. The awe in the eyes of the newcomers was palpable as they witnessed their new homes transform before them.

The schools within the Dome buzzed with activity, places of learning where knowledge was shared freely, and curiosity was nurtured. Children and adults alike discovered the wonders of Eloxonian science and the rich history of Earth, a curriculum designed to foster understanding and unity.

Life within the Dome was a symphony of harmony and peace. People from all walks of life, all corners of Earth, lived together, their differences celebrated, their common humanity embraced. The gardens were places of gathering, where stories were shared, and friendships were forged. The streams that wound through the landscape sang songs of renewal, and the air was filled with the scent of blooming flowers.

Within the Dome, a society was blossoming, one where every individual was empowered to pursue their passions and expand their horizons. The citizens, new arrivals from a world of limitations, discovered a place where barriers to education and opportunity had been dismantled. Here, they could be artisans, scholars, healers—whatever their hearts desired. The Dome's educational system, a nexus of Eloxonian knowledge and Earth's diverse cultures, offered learning experiences that were immersive and transformative.

Employment within the Dome was not a matter of necessity but of fulfillment. Jobs were aligned with skills and interests, ensuring that each person's work was a source of joy and pride. The community thrived as people engaged in tasks that resonated with their innate talents and newfound abilities, contributing to the greater good of all.

The vehicles provided to the inhabitants mirrored those of Eloxon 5, marvels of technology that glided above the ground, silent and efficient. They traversed the cities of the Dome, their graceful movements a dance of progress and harmony. The transportation network was a testament to the possibility of a world free from pollution and the chaos of congested streets.

As word of the Dome's utopia spread, the influx of people seeking entry grew. Some journeyed-on foot, determined to reach the promise of a better life. Others were ferried by the drones, their interiors equipped with screens that offered a glimpse into the life that awaited them. The images of green parks, smiling faces, and vibrant communities were a balm to weary souls, convincing many to embrace the change.

However, not all who wished to enter were deemed worthy by the Key. Families faced heart-wrenching decisions as some members were allowed passage while others were not. In acts of solidarity and love, some chose to stay behind, unwilling to fracture their family unit despite the allure of the Dome.

The Key's judgment, while ensuring the integrity of the Dome's society, also sowed seeds of division among those it turned away. It was a reminder that even in a world striving for perfection, difficult choices and sacrifices were inevitable.

Life within the Dome flourished as the population neared a million souls. Each new day was a testament to the society Eli had envisioned—a society where love and learning were the cornerstones of existence.

Families, reunited within the safety of the Dome, built lives filled with joy and purpose. The laughter of children filled the air, their days spent exploring the wonders of their new world. Couples walked hand in hand through the gardens, their love deepening in a place free from the fears that once shadowed their every step.

The sense of community was palpable, with neighbors sharing meals and stories under the stars. The Dome had become a melting pot of cultures and experiences, each individual contributing to the rich tapestry of life that wove through the city.

As the population grew, the need for expansion became apparent. Eli, ever the guardian of his people, knew that the Dome's boundaries could be extended with a mere thought. Yet, he chose to wait, to ensure that the society they were nurturing remained sustainable and true to the principles of harmony and balance.

In the city's museum, humans learned about life on Eloxon 5 through interactive exhibits and simulations. They walked through replicas of Eloxonian cities, touched the flora of alien worlds, and gazed upon the twin suns in virtual skies. The museum was not just a place of education but of experience, allowing the people of the Dome to understand the civilization that had inspired their sanctuary.

The schools were hives of activity, where the young and old alike discovered the secrets of the universe. The curriculum was diverse, covering the sciences and arts of both Earth and Eloxon 5. Students learned the value of empathy and the power of innovation, equipped with the knowledge to build a future that would honor both worlds.

The harmony within the Dome was a stark contrast to the turmoil that raged outside its borders. While the world's leaders plotted and schemed, the inhabitants of the Dome lived in peace, their lives a daily affirmation of the potential for a better humanity.

Chapter 24:

THE SIEGE OF THE DOME

In the shadowed halls of power, the world's military leaders and presidents convened, their faces etched with determination and unease. The Dome, a structure of peace and promise, had become the focal point of their fears and ambitions. Several countries, once rivals, now stood united in a singular purpose: to breach the sanctuary that Eli had created.

The plan was set in motion, a strategy gleaned from the minds of soldiers who believed they had penetrated the Dome. Their memories, altered by Eli's intervention, painted a picture of vulnerability—a Dome without weapons, without a military presence, ripe for the taking.

The commander-in-chief, flanked by his advisors and generals, issued the first command. "Initiate Operation Skyfall," he ordered, his voice a low rumble that resonated through the war room. The operation was a full-scale aerial assault, a show of might that they believed would crack the Dome's defenses.

Jets streaked across the sky, their payloads armed and ready. The roar of engines was a thunderous declaration of war against a foe they did not understand. As the first wave of strikes hit the Dome, the world watched with bated breath.

But the Dome stood unassailable. The rockets and bullets, designed to wreak havoc, were rendered impotent upon contact. They were absorbed into the force field, their destructive energy dissipated without a trace. The Dome, a creation of Eloxonian technology, was an immovable object facing the unstoppable force of Earth's military might.

Inside the Dome, life continued undisturbed. Children played in the gardens, families shared meals, and laughter echoed through the air. The inhabitants, shielded from the violence outside, remained blissfully unaware of the siege taking place.

Eli, Zandur, and Soloice, however, were acutely aware of the assault. From their vantage point, they watched as the jets made pass after pass, each attack as futile as the last. The siblings exchanged a look of sorrow, their disappointment in the world leaders' actions a heavy weight upon their hearts.

Eli's thoughts were a storm of strategy and concern. He had hoped that the display of the Dome's defenses would deter further aggression, that the leaders would see the futility of their actions. But the relentless attacks proved that fear and power were driving forces that blinded the leaders to reason.

As the night drew on, the attacks continued, a relentless barrage against the unyielding barrier of the Dome. Eli knew that the military's failure to penetrate the Dome would only escalate the situation. The leaders would not relent; they would regroup, rethink, and return with even more desperate measures.

The military's relentless assault on the Dome escalated as they deployed drones, each laden with explosives, in a desperate attempt to penetrate the barrier. The drones, like mechanical birds of prey, swarmed towards the Dome, their payloads intended to deliver destruction.

Yet, as they collided with the force field, the anticipated explosions were absent. The bombs, neutralized by the Dome's defenses, fell harmlessly to the desert floor, their threat extinguished as easily as a candle in the wind. The Dome remained untouched; its surface not even marred by the futile aggression of Earth's military might.

Undeterred, the military leaders commanded their next phase of attack. Chinook helicopters, retrofitted with flamethrowers capable of spewing infernos, took to the skies. The pilots, following their orders, positioned their aircraft above the Dome, unleashing torrents of fire upon it.

The flames, fierce and unyielding, roared like dragons set loose upon the world. Yet, against the Dome, they were but whispers of heat that dissipated upon contact. The force field absorbed the energy, its glow a silent testament to the futility of the attack.

Inside the Dome, Eli, Zandur, and Soloice observed the onslaught with a sense of sorrow for the blindness of the world's leaders. The inhabitants of the utopia, shielded from the chaos, continued their lives in peace, unaware of the battle being waged on their behalf.

Eli's restraint was a conscious choice, a hope that the leaders would see the error of their ways. He stood firm in his resolve, a beacon of nonviolence in the face of hostility. His desire was not to engage in battle but to open a dialogue, to show the world that there was another path—a path of peace and cooperation.

As the helicopters retreated, their fuel spent and weapons exhausted, the military regrouped, their frustration mounting. The Dome, a silent rebuke to their aggression, stood as a challenge to their authority and a question to their conscience.

When the attacks ceased and silence grew outside the dome Eli sent a telepathic message to the leaders of the world, his voice a calm amidst the storm. "We have withstood your attacks and remain unharmed," he communicated. "Let this be a sign that the way of violence is not the answer. I extend an invitation to talk, to find a peaceful resolution for the benefit of all."

The Siege of the Dome

The world leaders' council chamber was a cacophony of voices, each one clamoring over the next in a heated debate that would decide the fate of the Dome. The proposition on the table was dire: to deploy their nuclear arsenal against an entity they could not understand, could not control. The arguments oscillated between strategic offense and the moral implications of such an act, with some leaders vehemently opposing the use of atomic weaponry, citing the irreversible harm it could inflict upon the innocents and the environment.

Despite the opposition, the decision was made—a chilling consensus that sent ripples through the echelons of power. The order was given to prepare an atomic bomb, an act of aggression that would mark a point of no return.

Eli, having witnessed the leaders' deliberations through his extraordinary abilities, felt a cold dread settle in his chest. He relayed the grim decision to Zandur and Soloice, his voice tinged with a sorrow that mirrored the stormy skies outside the Dome. "We cannot allow the destruction they plan to unleash," he said, his words a solemn vow to protect the Earth he called home.

The siblings, united in their purpose, nodded in silent agreement. "We will do what we must," Zandur affirmed, his resolve as unyielding as the force field that encased their utopia. "For the good of the planet."

As the preparations for the nuclear strike began, Eli and his siblings readied themselves for the inevitable confrontation. The Dome, a bastion of peace, would soon be tested by the fires of war.

Eli, standing beneath the tranquil sky within the Dome, a stark contrast to the turbulent atmosphere beyond its borders. The beauty of the stars above served as a reminder of the sanctity of the world he was sworn to protect. As he gazed into the heavens, a single thought crystallized in his mind: "It must be done."

Chapter 25:
THE POWER UNLEASHED

---※---

As the military's preparations for a catastrophic assault on the Dome reached their zenith, the world's leaders were blind to the true extent of Eli's capabilities. They had not considered that Eli, with his extraordinary powers, could perceive their every move, their every intention.

The military's arsenal was formidable—two bombs, one atomic and the other hydrogen, each a harbinger of destruction. The leaders believed that deploying both would ensure at least one would breach the Dome's defenses. It was a gamble, a desperate ploy to sow confusion and fear.

But Eli, ever vigilant, had already discerned their plans. He refused to let their actions go unchallenged, to allow their weapons to threaten the planet he had sworn to protect. With a heavy heart, he decided to act before the bombs could be launched.

He reached out with his mind, his telepathic message resonating in the consciousness of every person outside the Dome. "I know what you have seen, what the world leaders have attempted against us," Eli's voice echoed across the globe. "I can tolerate the weapons used against the Dome, but they plan to unleash a force that endangers our entire world. This, I cannot permit."

Eli's words were a clarion call, a plea for the people to see the truth behind the actions of their leaders. He spoke of his attempts at peace, of his efforts to save humanity from the destructive path laid out by those in power.

With resolve steeling his every word, Eli declared an end to the old ways. "Today, it ends. Your way of living is at an end," he proclaimed. And with that, he stepped out from the Dome, his hands raised to the sky, channeling the energy of the Dome and its people.

A roar escaped him as he unleashed a telepathic wave that rippled around the world. It was an EMP of unprecedented power, a surge that extinguished all electricity, all power outside the Dome. Batteries drained, phones died, and radio transmissions fell silent. The rockets, primed for destruction, were rendered inert, their facilities plunged into darkness.

Eli's final message was a somber reminder of the cost of power and the price of peace. "In order to maintain peace and limit the damage to this world, I have taken away what you crave most—your power."

The Power Unleashed

In the wake of Eli's decisive action, the world leaders found themselves in a state of disarray. The once-mighty figures, accustomed to control and command, were reduced to shadows of their former selves, scrambling in the darkness that had enveloped their world.

The war rooms and command centers, hubs of strategy and authority, were now silent tombs. Screens that had flickered with data and maps lay dormant; the lifeblood of information cut off by Eli's EMP-like blast. The leaders, stripped of their technological dominion, were left blind and impotent.

Panic seeped into the hearts of those who had wielded power with such confidence. Generals and advisors, presidents and prime ministers—all were united in their fear, a stark contrast to the unity they had lacked when plotting against the Dome. Their voices, once so firm and decisive, now trembled with uncertainty.

"Everything's gone," one general muttered, his hand sliding over a dead console. "Our communications, our defenses—how could this happen?"

The president, his composure shaken, tried to rally his team. "We need to get systems back online," he insisted, though the quiver in his voice betrayed his anxiety. "There must be a way to counteract this."

But the truth was clear: Eli had dismantled the very foundation of their power without firing a shot or spilling a drop of blood. The world outside the Dome, so dependent on the web of technology that had ensnared it, was now caught in a web of its own making.

As emergency protocols failed to activate and backup generators sputtered to silence, the realization dawned on the leaders that they were witnessing the end of an era. The weapons they had brandished so boldly were now relics in a world that had changed in the blink of an eye.

Eli returned to the dome and was met by Zandur and Soloice. Both affirming the choices Eli had made. Eli looked at them and told them of his plan to go out into the world. "Traveling to the dome will become even more dangerous now that there is no power," Eli stated. "I must go to ensure the safety of the world."

Eli's resolve to venture out into the world was met with understanding and a shared sense of duty by his siblings. They knew the risks, the panic that would ensue in a world plunged into darkness. Yet, they also knew the importance of guiding those lost in the night to the sanctuary of the Dome.

As they prepared to depart, the sudden screech tore through the silence of the night, a sound that resonated with an ominous frequency. It was a sound that only Eli and his siblings could hear, a clarion call that spoke of an arrival from beyond.

Rushing out of the ship, they looked skyward, their enhanced vision piercing through the protective barrier of the Dome. There, against the backdrop of the cosmos, a white hole had opened, and from its depths emerged a

The Power Unleashed

ship of colossal proportions—a vessel that dwarfed even the grandeur of the Dome.

Eli's confusion was mirrored in the faces of Zandur and Soloice. The ship was familiar, a haunting memory from his journey back to Earth. It was a specter that had lingered at the edges of his consciousness, now made manifest in the skies above.

The siblings exchanged a knowing glance, a silent acknowledgment of the ship's identity. It was a piece of Eloxon 5, a remnant of the world they had left behind. But its presence here, now, was a puzzle that demanded answers.

Eli's plea for understanding was cut short by the voice of Mother, a voice that carried with it the weight of worlds. "I am disappointed, my son," she spoke, her words a cascade of emotion that washed over him.

In an instant, Eli's world went dark, his consciousness slipping away into the void of sleep. The last thing he saw was the concern etched on the faces of his siblings, the last thing he felt was the cold touch of disappointment from the world he had called home.

Chapter 26:
THE COUNCIL OF SHADOWS

On Eloxon 5, days before the tumult on Earth reached its crescendo, life proceeded with its usual tranquility. But in the heart of the planet, within the chambers of the Council of Elders, a storm of a different kind was brewing.

The Elders, ancient beings of wisdom and power, convened in a room that pulsed with the life force of the planet. At the head of the table sat Mother, her visage serene yet troubled. The topic at hand was Earth, a world teetering on the brink of self-destruction, and the role of her son, Eli, in its fate.

"Is he fulfilling his duties?" one Elder asked, his voice echoing through the chamber. "Will he do what is necessary?"

Mother's response was laced with concern. "Eli will do as he has been taught," she affirmed. "But I fear he harbors doubts. He saw the ship before he returned to Earth, and it has sown seeds of mistrust in his mind."

The revelation cast a shadow over the council. The ship, a harbinger of Eloxon 5's darker intentions, was not meant for Eli's eyes—not yet. It was the instrument of a plan long in the making, a plan that hinged on Eli's decision.

"I should have been more forthcoming with him," Mother confessed. "But his brother and sister are with him. They will guide him back to the path should he stray."

The council murmured their agreement, their faith in the siblings unwavering. Yet, beneath their words lay an undercurrent of anticipation. The destruction of humanity was a prospect they viewed with clinical detachment. To them, humans were but vermin, creatures too consumed by their baser instincts to warrant salvation.

The Elders spoke of Earth with a cold calculus. "It is a beautiful planet, wasted on those who inhabit it," another elder spoke. "Eli must see this. He must understand that the survival of Eloxon 5, the expansion of our civilization, takes precedence."

Mother nodded, her eyes reflecting the cold stars outside. "He will see the truth," she said. "He must. The future of our people, the continuation of our way of life, depends on it."

Mother emerged from the chamber of the Elders, her mind a tempest of concern and frustration. She retreated to the solitude of her palace, seeking the clarity that only meditation could provide. As she delved into the depths of her consciousness, she extended her awareness to her children, Zandur and Soloice, who were with Eli on Earth.

Their minds were a tumult of conflict and guilt, their thoughts interwoven with doubt about the mission. They communicated in hushed mental tones, their unease with Eli's actions palpable even across the vastness of space. Mother's breath caught in her throat as she realized the gravity of their words—Eli had activated the Dome.

This was not the plan. The Dome was meant to be a temporary measure, a means to an end, not the end itself. Mother's fury simmered beneath the surface as she shifted her focus to Eli's mind, seeking answers.

What she found was Eli, engaged in a mental dialogue with the world, extolling the virtues of the utopia he had created within the Dome. He spoke of safety, of a new beginning, of a world free from the corruption and decay that plagued Earth. His intentions were pure, his desire to save humanity genuine.

Mother's fury boiled over. This was a deviation from the path they had set for Eli. He was meant to return to Eloxon 5, to bring about the decision that would ensure their planet's future. Instead, he was offering salvation to a species they had deemed beyond redemption.

She pondered where she had gone wrong. In her last glimpse into Eli's mind before his departure, she had been confident that he understood his duty. She had not anticipated his empathy for humans would outweigh the cold logic of their plan.

Eli's actions posed a dilemma. If he continued on this course, the opportunity to claim Earth for Eloxon 5 might slip through their fingers. The humans, whom the Elders viewed as a blight upon a precious world, were being given a chance to thrive—a chance Mother and the Elders believed they did not deserve.

Mother's urgency was palpable as she commanded the team preparing the ship for Earth. Time was of the essence, and each moment wasted could spell unforeseen consequences for their plans. The team, initially projecting a week's time for readiness, acquiesced to her insistence on a couple of days. The time dilation between Earth and Eloxon 5 was a variable they could not afford to overlook. "Ready the Alpha weapon!" Mother ordered.

The mention of the Alpha weapon sent a ripple of confusion through the team. It was a tool of last resort, a nanotech marvel capable of targeting and eradicating specific DNA sequences. One member's question reflected the team's unease, but Mother's response was unyielding—it was the will of Eloxon 5.

Obedience overrode hesitation, and the team set to work on the Alpha weapon. It was a grim task, the implications of its use a heavy burden. The weapon, designed to act swiftly and decisively, could extinguish the human race while sparing the planet and its other inhabitants.

Mother's internal monologue revealed the depth of her resolve. The Alpha weapon was, in her eyes, the most ethical solution to the human problem. It was a clean cut, a way to remove humanity from the equation without the messy collateral damage of conventional warfare.

Mother's urgency did not wane as she informed the Elders of Eloxon 5 about the acceleration of their plans. Their response was unanimous and immediate: make haste. The gravity of the situation on Earth demanded swift action, and Mother was all too aware of the stakes at play.

With the ship's preparations underway, Mother sought solace in meditation, her mind reaching across the cosmos to Earth. The visions that unfolded before her were a tapestry of conflict and harmony. She saw the military's relentless assault on the Dome, the futile attempts to penetrate its sanctuary with fire and steel. Yet, within the Dome, life blossomed—a stark contrast to the chaos outside its walls.

The sight of Eli and his siblings, Zandur and Soloice, living among the humans, sharing in their joys and sorrows, stirred a whirlwind of emotions within Mother. Confusion clouded her judgment, the lines between duty and empathy blurred by the unexpected bonds forming between her children and the inhabitants of Earth.

The discord among humans, their violence against one another to prevent access to the Dome, only served to reinforce Mother's resolve. The decision to eradicate humanity, once a matter of cold logic, now seemed a necessary act of preservation. The humans' own actions justified the dark verdict she had reached.

Yet, as she attempted to bridge the mental gap with Eli and his siblings, a barrier prevented her from making a full connection. She could see through their eyes, witness the past and present, but the future remained shrouded in mystery.

Mother's frustration grew as she grappled with the limitations of her reach. The inability to communicate directly with her children left her with a sense of helplessness, a feeling foreign to a being of her power and stature.

Chapter 27:
THE WILL OF ELOXON 5

---※---

Days had turned into nights, and nights into days, as the people of Eloxon 5 worked tirelessly to ready the ship for its crucial journey. The time had come, and with a sense of urgency that permeated the air, Mother commanded the crew to prepare for immediate departure to Earth.

Mother's presence at the launch bay was met with surprise from the crew, who had not expected her to accompany them. "Mother, are you coming with us?" they asked, their voices tinged with confusion. Her response was clear and authoritative, "The mission is urgent, and I am taking charge of the ship." The crew bowed their heads in respect, their voices united, "If it is the will of Eloxon 5."

With Mother at the helm, the ship—a behemoth of technology and power—launched into the skies, ascending into the vastness of space. The black hole portal, a gateway between worlds, was activated, and Mother gave the command to enter. The crew braced themselves as the ship approached the event horizon, the boundary between the known and the unknown.

In her quarters, Mother settled into meditation, her mind reaching across the cosmos to establish a connection with her children. The visions that came to her were troubling. She saw the Earth's military preparing to unleash nuclear devastation upon the Dome. She witnessed Eli's countermeasure, an EMP attack that rendered all electricity inert—a move that aligned with her own intentions to ensure no harm would come to the planet.

But it was Eli's message to the world that gave her pause. His words, filled with love and empathy, were a stark contrast to the will of Eloxon 5. Mother knew that Eli's compassion for humanity would clash with their decision to eradicate the species. She understood, with a heavy heart, that her son might never condone the actions they deemed necessary.

As she emerged from her meditative state, Mother's resolve was unshaken. She knew what she had to do. The fate of Eloxon 5 and Earth hung in the balance, and she was prepared to make the hard choices, to carry out the will of her people—even if it meant standing against her own son.

As the ship emerged from the black hole, the crew was bathed in the brilliant white light of transition.

THE WILL OF ELOXON 5

For some, it was a moment of profound awe, their first journey through the cosmic gateway. For others, it was a familiar process, one that demanded focus and adherence to their mission.

Mother, standing at the helm, felt the resurgence of her connection to her children. The bond that had been stretched thin across the void of space now enveloped her with its full strength. She sent out a mental signal, a beacon that pierced through the vastness to reach Zandur, Soloice, and Eli.

The siblings, upon receiving Mother's call, were struck with a mix of emotions. Confusion and concern clouded their minds as they listened to her voice. Mother's disappointment was a palpable force, a wave of disapproval that washed over them.

"Eli, my son, I am disappointed," Mother's voice resonated within their thoughts. Her words were a sharp contrast to the peace of the Dome, a discordant note in the symphony of their new life.

Without warning, Mother's presence invaded Eli's mind with the precision of a surgeon's blade. She delved into the depths of his consciousness, and with a gentle but firm touch, she induced a deep slumber. Eli's body went limp, his thoughts fading into darkness as he succumbed to the forced rest.

In the depths of space, aboard the colossal ship aimed for Earth, Mother's command to ready the weapon echoed with a sense of finality. The crew, their fingers dancing over the controls, activated the weapon—a giant ring designed to unleash nanobots upon the Earth, programmed to seek and destroy human DNA.

Zandur and Soloice, Mother's other children, cried out in mental protest. Their voices, laden with emotion, reached out to Mother. "This is not the way of Eloxon 5," they pleaded. "Humans are not beyond redemption. Peace is still possible."

But Mother, her resolve as unyielding as the metal of the ship, ignored their pleas. She believed in the necessity of her actions, convinced that humanity posed a threat to the sanctity of Eloxon 5. The weapon hummed to life, its systems calculating the presence of humans below.

As the countdown began, Zandur severed the mental connection with Mother and took control of the crew member handling the weapon. His superior mental strength allowed him to override the crew member's actions, attempting to render the weapon inert. But Mother, sensing the betrayal, cast the crew member into a forced slumber and reactivated the weapon.

The countdown continued, and Soloice worked frantically to rouse Eli from his induced sleep. As the numbers climbed—seventy percent, eighty percent—Eli began to stir. At ninety percent, he awoke, his mind instantly flooded with the knowledge of the impending doom.

With the countdown at ninety five percent, Eli leaped to his feet, his hand pressed to his temple as he sought to wrest control from Mother. At one hundred percent, as Mother's finger hovered over the button to release the weapon, she found herself paralyzed, unable to complete the action.

Eli had taken control, his mental prowess overpowering even Mother's will. His siblings exchanged looks of relief and pride, their faith in Eli validated. Mother's mental screams filled the connection, demanding her release, but Eli held firm.

The crew, noticing Mother's stillness, rushed to assist her, but Eli's power was absolute. With a thought, he put them all into a deep sleep, their bodies slumping to the ground.

Eli's siblings revealed the truth to him: he was imbued with abilities beyond any Eloxonian protector, crafted to be Earth's decider. His mental strength was unmatched, a gift that now stood between humanity and annihilation.

Mother's fury was a storm in their minds, her warnings of consequences a distant thunder. But Eli, looking amidst the sleeping crew, knew that the fate of two worlds rested in his hands.

With mother still frozen by Elis will. Eli and his siblings boarded his ship and launched in the air through the dome to the ship above them.

Eli, with a heavy heart, watched as Mother's figure receded from the control panel, her form still frozen by his will. Zandur swiftly moved to deactivate the weapon once more, his fingers flying over the controls with a practiced ease. The hum of the weapon powering down was a symphony of relief that echoed through the silent ship.

Mother's voice, filled with contempt, broke the silence. She lamented her affection for Eli, expressing regret that he had ever set foot on Eloxon 5. Eli, his heart aching with the weight of her words, offered his apologies for disrupting her plans. He implored her to see the beauty and goodness of Earth, flooding her mind with memories of joy, love, and harmony among its inhabitants.

Tears welled in Mother's eyes, a response to the flood of human emotions that Eli shared with her. Yet, her resolve remained unbroken. She insisted that the mission must be completed, that the eradication of humanity was a necessary act for the greater good of Eloxon 5.

Eli, bewildered by Mother's unwavering stance, questioned the very nature of the Key. "Isn't this evil?" he asked, his voice echoing with confusion. "Shouldn't the Key have prevented this at birth?"

Zandur and Soloice exchanged troubled glances, their own doubts mirroring Eli's. They concurred that mother's actions were not reflective of their people's values, that her refusal to engage in reason or debate was a departure from the way of Eloxon 5.

With the weapon now inactive, the siblings stood united, their bond strengthened in the face of Mother's darkness. Eli called upon the ship's computer, seeking confirmation of the Key's presence. The computer's voice, neutral and precise, affirmed that the Key was indeed woven into the fabric of all Eloxonian creations.

Eli's request for the Key to analyze Mother was met with a chilling response. The computer detailed a litany of sins—betrayal, jealousy, corruption—attributes that should have been purged by the Key's judgment. The siblings were stunned. How had Mother evaded the Key's justice?

The computer's answer was a revelation that shook them to their core. The Elders of Eloxon 5, including Mother, were immune to the laws of the Key. They existed above the moral safeguards that governed their society, a privilege that allowed darkness to fester in the shadows of power.

Eli and his siblings, Zandur and Soloice, stood in the control room of the ship, their hearts heavy with the revelation of the Elders' betrayal. The disappointment was a bitter pill to swallow, the realization that the darkness they sought to eradicate in humanity was mirrored in the leaders of their own world.

Eli, feeling a sense of abandonment that echoed through the void, took control of the situation. With a mere thought, Mother's body relaxed into a deep slumber, her form guided gently to the ground by Eli's mental embrace. The decision to return to Eloxon 5 was put on hold; they could not turn their backs on the deceit that had unfolded.

Zandur, ever the strategist, proposed a bold move. "You can reveal the truth to our people," he said to Eli. "Show them what has transpired here, the corruption that has taken root in our leadership."

Eli, though powerful, doubted the reach of his abilities. Could he truly connect with every mind across the expanse of space? His siblings' faith in him was unwavering. "We believe in you," Soloice affirmed. "You have the strength to do this."

With their encouragement, Eli reached out with his mind, his consciousness stretching across the cosmos. He found the thread that connected him to Eloxon 5 and followed it, his presence passing through the black hole and into the minds of his people.

The connection was made, and Eli's will coursed through the collective consciousness of Eloxon 5. Every citizen, every Elder, felt the weight of his revelations. The truth of Mother's actions, the immunity of the Elders to the Key's judgment, was laid bare for all to see.

The people of Eloxon 5 were now aware of the shadows that lurked behind the facade of their society. The future was uncertain, but one thing was clear: the veil of deception had been lifted, and the path forward would be one of reckoning and change.

Chapter 28:
THE END OF AN ERA

Eli and his siblings stood resolute in their decision; the ship that had brought them from Eloxon 5 would not see their home again. It was a relic of a past that no longer aligned with the future they envisioned for Earth. "The weapon must be destroyed," Zandur declared, his voice echoing the finality of their choice.

With a command to the ship's computer, Eli initiated the deactivation and destruction of the weapon. The nanobots, once a threat to humanity, turned upon themselves, consuming the very mechanism of their creation. It was a poetic end to a device designed for annihilation.

Mother, still in slumber, was to be returned to Eloxon 5, along with the crew. They deserved to face the consequences of their actions, to answer for the part they played in the near-catastrophe. Zandur and Soloice carefully placed them in a rescue pod, setting its course back to their planet.

As Eli opened the black hole portal, the rescue pod slipped through, embarking on its journey across the stars. The fate of Mother and the crew was now in the hands of the Elders and the people of Eloxon 5.

With the future of Earth at stake, Eli gave the command to the ship's computer to activate self-destruction. A countdown began, the digital voice of the computer announcing the seconds as they ticked away. "sixty seconds until self-destruction," it intoned, a solemn countdown to the end of an era.

Eli, Zandur, and Soloice boarded their smaller ship, casting one last glance at the behemoth that had been their vessel from another world. As they flew towards Earth, the ship behind them imploded, collapsing in upon itself in a silent, brilliant display. In less than a minute, it was gone, leaving no trace of its existence, no mark upon the cosmos.

The return to the Dome was a quiet affair. Eli, Zandur, and Soloice descended back into their sanctuary, the events of the night known only to them. The world outside, shrouded in darkness from the EMP blast, remained oblivious to the near-catastrophe that had unfolded above.

Inside the Dome, life continued in blissful ignorance. The sky within showed no signs of the conflict that had raged beyond its protective barrier. The stars twinkled peacefully, and the gentle hum of the Dome's energy resonated with the promise of safety and harmony.

Eli, however, knew that silence was not an option. The world needed to understand the magnitude of what had occurred—the threat that had loomed over them and the lengths to which he had gone to protect not just the Dome, but the entire planet.

With a heavy heart, Eli prepared to share the night's events with the inhabitants of the Dome and the world beyond. He hoped that the truth would serve as a catalyst for change, that it would awaken the people to the reality of their leaders' actions and the potential for a different path.

Eli gathered the inhabitants of the Dome, his voice echoing with the gravity of recent events. "My friends," he began, "we have been through a trial by fire, unseen and unknown until now. A ship from Eloxon 5, my birthplace, came with a weapon capable of eradicating all human life on Earth."

The crowd murmured, the weight of his words settling upon them like a shroud. "This weapon, known as the Alpha, was designed to target human DNA specifically," Eli continued. "It would have left our planet intact while removing humanity from existence."

A sense of disbelief rippled through the Dome. Eli's siblings, Zandur and Soloice, stood by his side, their expressions solemn. "We stopped it," Eli assured them. "We chose to protect life, to uphold the values we cherish within this Dome."

Eli, understanding the need for transparency and the power of shared experience, decided to reveal the truth to the rest of humanity. He knew that for them to make an informed decision about coming to the Dome, they needed to witness the events as they had unfolded.

With the same mental prowess that allowed him to connect with the people of Eloxon 5, Eli reached out to the minds of those outside the Dome. He cast a wide telepathic net, inviting them to see through his eyes, to feel what he felt, and to understand the choices he had made.

The people of Earth closed their eyes and found themselves immersed in Eli's memories. They saw the ship from Eloxon 5 looming in space, the threat of the Alpha weapon, and the decisive moment when Eli chose to protect humanity. They felt the tension of the confrontation with Mother, the release of the EMP disabling the world's power, and the destruction of the ship that could have ended their existence.

As the vision faded, the people were left with a profound sense of what had been at stake. Eli's voice, gentle yet firm, spoke to them once more. "Now you know the truth," he said. "The choice is yours. The Dome is open to all who seek a new beginning, a life of peace and unity. Come and join us, and together, we will forge a future where the mistakes of the past are lessons for a brighter tomorrow."

As the truth of the night's events spread across the globe, a shift in perception began to take hold. The people of Earth, once divided by fear and uncertainty, now clamored for the safety and promise of the Dome. Eli could sense their desperation, their voices a chorus of hope reaching out for salvation.

The End of an Era

In response, Eli dispatched his fleet of drones, each one a vessel of refuge, to every corner of the world. They were beacons of light cutting through the darkness, offering safe passage to those who sought a new beginning within the Dome.

Within the sanctuary of the Dome, the atmosphere was one of concern and curiosity. The inhabitants, having witnessed the near-destruction of their species, sought reassurance about their place in the universe. They bombarded Eli with questions, their eyes reflecting a mixture of fear and trust.

Eli addressed the people, his voice a steady presence amidst the storm of worry. "The actions taken against us were the will of a select few," he explained. "They do not represent the entirety of Eloxon 5. I will reach out to my home planet and confirm that peace will be maintained."

The people listened, taking solace in Eli's words. His promise to make contact with Eloxon 5 was a ray of hope, a potential bridge between worlds that could foster understanding rather than conflict.

The world outside the Dome was changing, its people uniting with a common goal. The Dome stood as a symbol of what could be achieved when fear was cast aside in favor of hope. Eli's journey was far from over, but he was ready to face whatever challenges lay ahead, for the sake of both Earth and Eloxon 5.